The
Company
of the
Noble Seven

The Company of the Noble Seven

Ralph Connor

Edited by Timothy McCullough

THOMAS NELSON PUBLISHERS
Nashville • Atlanta • London • Vancouver

Copyright © 1996 by Timothy McCullough

All rights reserved. Written permission must be secured from the publisher to use or reproduce any part of this book, except for brief quotations in critical reviews or articles.

Published in Nashville, Tennessee, by Thomas Nelson, Inc., Publishers, and distributed in Canada by Word Communications, Ltd., Richmond, British Columbia.

The Bible version used in this publication is the KING JAMES VERSION.

Library of Congress Cataloging-in-Publication Data

Connor, Ralph, 1860–1937.
   The Company of the Noble Seven / Ralph Connor : edited by Timothy McCullough:
     p. cm.
   Rev. ed. of: The sky pilot. 1970
   "A Janet Thoma book."
   ISBN 0-7852-7578-9
   1. Clergy—Canadian Rockies (B.C. and Alta.)—Fiction.
I. McCullough, Timothy. II. Connor, Ralph, 1860–1937. Sky pilot. III. Title.
PR9199.2.G6C66 1996
813'.52—dc20   95-52358
                                                                       CIP

Printed in the United States of America.
1 2 3 4 5 6 — 01 00 99 98 97 96

*To my Dad, Calvin McCullough,
whose love of good books made this possible.*

Contents

Acknowledgments ix
Preface xi

1. The Foothills Country 1
2. The Company of the Noble Seven 11
3. The Coming of the Pilot 21
4. The Pilot's Measure 29
5. First Blood 37
6. His Second Wind 49
7. The Last of the Permit Sundays 57
8. The Pilot's Grip 67
9. Gwen 81
10. Gwen's First Prayers 95
11. Gwen's Challenge 109
12. Gwen's Canyon 121
13. The Canyon Flowers 133
14. Bill's Bluff 145
15. Bill's Partner 159
16. Bill's Financing 167
17. How the Pinto Sold 175
18. The Lady Charlotte 183
19. Through Gwen's Window 189
20. How Bill Favored "Home-Grown Industries" 201
21. How Bill Hit the Trail 209

22. How the Swan Creek Church Was Opened   219
23. The Pilot's Last Port   223

About the Author   237
About the Editor   239

Acknowledgments

Thanks to the editors and staff at Janet Thoma Books for their hard work on this project.

Special thanks to Hazel Gaines, Amy Glass, Greg Holland, and Jim Reimann for their advice and encouragement.

Preface

The measure of a man's power to help his brother is a measure of his love and a measure of the faith he has that, at last, the good will win. With this love that seeks not its own and this faith that grips the heart of things, he goes out to meet destiny, but not defeat.

This story is of the people of the Foothill Country, those hills that lie in the eastern shadow of the Canadian Rockies. It is the story of those men who left homes of comfort, often of luxury, because of the stirring in them to be and to do something worthy. It is also the story of those others who, outcast from their kind, sought to find in those remote and lonely valleys a spot where they could forget and be forgotten.

The waving skyline of the Foothills was the

boundary of their outlook upon life. Here they were safe from the world's view, freed from the restraints of society, and denied the gentling influences of home and the sweet inspiration of a good woman's face. With this new freedom beating in their hearts and ears, many rode the wild trail to the brink of destruction.

This story is also about a man with vision, who came to the people of the Foothills with a firm purpose to play the brother's part. By his love of them and by his faith in them, he sought to help them understand that life is priceless and that it is good to be a man.

The term "Sky Pilot" is American slang for clergyman or chaplain. It first came into common written usage in the early 1880s.

1

The Foothills Country

The invitation from Jack Dale, a distant cousin, to spend a summer with him on his ranch in South Alberta came in the nick of time. I was wild to go. My guardian hesitated, but no other opportunity presented itself, so he agreed that I could not get into more trouble by going than by staying. And so it was that, in the early summer of one of the eighties, I found myself attached to a Hudson's Bay Company freight train, making our way from a little railway town in Montana toward the Canadian border.

Our train consisted of six wagons, fourteen yoke of oxen, and three cayuses, all in the charge of a French half-breed and his son, a lad of about sixteen. Our progress was slow, but every hour of the long day was full of new delights for me.

On the evening of the third day we reached the Line Stopping Place, where Jack Dale met us. I remember how I admired the easy grace with which he sailed down upon us in the loose-jointed cowboy style, swinging his own bronco and the little cayuse he was leading for me into the circle of wagons, careless of the ropes and freight and other impediments. He flung himself off before his bronco had come to a stop, and he gave me a grip that made me sure of my welcome. It was years since he had seen a man from home, and the eager joy in his eyes told of long days and nights of lonely yearning for the old days and the old faces. After my two-year stay among these hills, I came to understand the strange longings that waken some days in a man, longings that make his heart grow sick.

When supper was over we gathered about the little fire, while Jack and the half-breed smoked and talked. I lay on my back looking up at the stars in the deep blue of the cloudless sky, and listened in contented delight to the chat between Jack and the driver. Now and then I asked a question, but not too often. It is a listening silence that draws tales from a Western man, not vexing questions. This much I had learned already from my three days' travel. So I lay and listened, and the tales of that night were mingled with the warm evening lights and the pale stars and the thoughts of home that Jack's coming seemed to bring.

Next morning before sunup we had broken camp and were ready for our fifty-mile ride. There was a slight drizzle of rain, and though rain and shine were alike to him, Jack insisted that I should wear my mackintosh. This garment was quite new and had a loose cape that rustled as I moved toward my cayuse. He was an ugly-looking little animal, with more white in his eye than I cared to see. Altogether, I was not drawn toward him, nor him to me, apparently. For as I took him by the bridle he snorted and sidled about with great swiftness and stood facing me with his feet planted firmly in front of him as if prepared to reject all overtures of any kind. I tried to approach him with soothing words, but he persistently backed away until we stood looking at each other at the greatest distance of his outstretched neck and my outstretched arm. At this point Jack came to my assistance, got the pony by the other side of the bridle, and held him fast till I got into position to mount. Taking a firm grip of the horn of the Mexican saddle, I threw my leg over his back. The next instant I was flying over his head. My only emotion was one of surprise; the thing was so unexpected. I had fancied myself a fair rider, having had experience on farmers' colts, but this was something quite new. The half-breed stood looking on, mildly interested; Jack was faintly smiling, but the boy was grinning with delight.

"I'll take the little beast," said Jack.

But the grinning boy braced me up, and I replied as carelessly as my shaking voice would allow: "Oh, I guess I'll manage him," and once more got into position. But no sooner had I gotten into the saddle than the pony sprang straight up into the air and lit with his back curved into a bow, his four legs gathered together and so absolutely rigid that the shock made my teeth rattle. It was my first experience of "bucking." Then the little brute went seriously to work to get rid of the rustling, flapping thing on his back. He would back steadily for some seconds, then, with two or three forward plunges, he would stop as if shot and spring straight into the upper air, lighting with back curved and legs rigid as iron. Then he would walk on his hind legs for a few steps, then throw himself with amazing rapidity to one side and again proceed to buck with vicious diligence.

"Stick to him!" yelled Jack, through bouts of laughter. "You'll make him sick before long."

I remember thinking that unless his insides were somewhat more delicately arranged than his external appearance would lead one to suppose, the chances were that the little brute would be the last to succumb to sickness. To make matters worse, a particularly wild jump threw my cape up over my head, so that I was in complete darkness. Now he had me at his mercy, and he knew no pity. He kicked and plunged and reared and bucked, now on his front legs, now on his hind legs, often on his knees, while I, in the darkness, could only cling to the horn of the saddle. At last, in one of the gleams of light that penetrated the folds of my enveloping cape, I found that the horn had slipped to his side, so the next time he came to his knees I threw myself off. I want to make this point clear, for, from the expression of triumph on the face of the grinning boy, and his praise for the pony, I gathered that he scored a win for the cayuse. Without pause that little brute continued for some seconds to buck and plunge even after my dismounting, as if he were a machine that must run down before it could stop.

By this time I was sick and badly shaken, but the triumphant shouts and laughter of the boy and the complacent smiles on the faces of Jack and the half-breed stirred my wrath. I tore off the cape and, having put the saddle right, seized Jack's riding whip and, disregarding his warnings, sprang on my steed once more. Before he could make up his mind as to his line of action, I plied him so vigorously with the rawhide that he set off over the prairie at full gallop. In a few minutes the pony came back to the camp quite subdued, to the boy's great disappointment and to my own great surprise. Jack was highly pleased, and even the stolid face of the half-breed showed satisfaction.

"Don't think I put this up on you," Jack said. "It was that cape. He ain't used to such frills. But it was a circus," he added, going off into a fit of laughter, "worth five dollars any day."

"You bet!" said the half-breed. "Dat's make pretty beeg fun, eh?"

It seemed to me that it depended somewhat upon the point of view, but I merely agreed with him, only too glad to be so well out of the fight.

All day we followed the trail that wound along the shoulders of the round-topped hills or down their long slopes into the wide, grassy valleys. Here and there the valleys were cut through by ravines through which ran swift, blue-gray rivers, clear and icy cold, while from the hilltops we caught glimpses of little lakes covered with wildfowl that shrieked and squawked and splashed, careless of danger. Now and then we saw what made a black spot against the green of the prairie, and Jack told me it was a rancher's shack. How remote from the great world, and how lonely it seemed—this little black shack among these many hills.

I shall never forget the summer evening when Jack and I rode into Swan Creek. I say into—but the village was almost entirely one of imagination, in that it consisted of the Stopping Place, a long log building, a story and a half high, with stables behind, and the store in which the post office was kept and over which the owner lived.

But the site was one of great beauty. On one side the prairie rambled down from the hills and then stretched away in tawny levels into the misty purple at the horizon; on the other it clambered over the round, sunny tops to the dim blue of the mountains beyond.

In the vastness of these hills, where it is difficult to reach absolute values, we are forced to hold things relatively, and in contrast with the long, lonely miles of our ride during the day, these townhouses, with their outbuildings, seemed a center of life.

Jack glanced at the horses tied to the rail that ran along in front of the Stopping Place. "Hello!" he said. "I guess the Noble Seven are in town."

"And who are they?" I asked.

"Oh," he replied, with a shrug, "they are the *elite* of Swan Creek; and, by Jove," he added, "this must be Permit Night."

"What does that mean?" I asked, as we rode up toward the tie rail.

"Well," said Jack, in a low tone, for some men were standing about the door, "you see, this is a Prohibition country, but when one of the boys feels as if he were going to have a spell of sickness he gets a permit to bring in a few gallons for medicinal purposes; and of course, the other boys being similarly exposed, he invites them to assist him in taking preventive measures. And," added Jack, with a solemn wink, "it is remarkable, in a healthy country like this, how many epidemics come near ketching us."

And with this mystifying explanation we joined the mysterious Company of the Noble Seven.

2

The Company of the Noble Seven

As we were dismounting, the cries, "Hello, Jack!" "How do, Dale?" "Hello, old Smoke!" in the heartiest of tones, made me see that my cousin was a favorite with the men grouped about the door. Jack simply nodded in reply and then presented me in due form. "My tenderfoot cousin from back East society," he said with a flourish.

I was surprised at the grace of the bows made me by these roughly-dressed, wild-looking fellows. I might have been in a London drawing room. I was at once put at ease by the friendliness of their greeting, for upon Jack's introduction, I was admitted at once into their circle, which, to a tenderfoot, was usually closed.

What a hardy-looking lot they were! Brown, spare, sinewy, and hard as nails, they appeared like soldiers back from a hard campaign. They moved and spoke with an easy, careless air of almost lazy indifference, but their eyes had a trick of looking straight at you, cool and fearless, making you feel that these men were fit and ready for anything.

That night I was initiated into the Company of the Noble Seven—but of the ceremony I regret to say I retain but an indistinct memory; for they drank as they rode, hard and long, and it was only Jack's care that got me safely home that night.

The Company of the Noble Seven was the dominant social force in the Swan Creek country. Indeed, it was the only social force Swan Creek knew. Originally consisting of seven young fellows of the best blood of Britain, "banded together for purposes of mutual improvement and social enjoyment," it had changed its character during the years, but not its name. First, membership was extended to include "approved colonials," such as Jack Dale and "others of kindred spirit," under which head, I suppose, the two cowboys from the Ashley Ranch, Hi Kendal and "Bronco" Bill—no one knew and no one asked Bronco's other name—were admitted. Then its purposes gradually limited themselves to those of a social nature, chiefly in the line of poker playing and whisky drinking.

Well-born in that atmosphere of culture mingled with common sense and a certain high chivalry that surrounds the stately homes of Britain, these young men, freed from the restraint of custom and surrounding, soon shed all that was superficial in their makeup. The West discovered and revealed the man in them, sometimes to their honor, often to their shame.

The chief of the Company was the Honorable Fred Ashley, of the Ashley Ranch, sometime of Ashley Court, England—a big, good-natured man with a magnificent physique, a good income from home, and a beautiful wife, the Lady Charlotte, daughter of a noble English family. At the Ashley Ranch the traditions of Ashley Court were preserved as far as possible. The Honorable Fred appeared at the wolf hunts in riding breeches and top boots, with hunting crop and English saddle, while in the house the customs of the English home were observed. It was characteristic, however, of Western life that Ashley's two cowboys, Hi Kendal and Bronco Bill, felt themselves quite his social equals, though in the presence of his beautiful stately wife they confessed that they "rather weakened." Ashley was a good fellow through and through, well up to his work as a cattleman and too much of a gentleman to feel or assert any superiority of station. He had the largest ranch in the country and was one of the few men making money.

Ashley's chief friend and most frequent companion was a man whom they called "the Duke." No one knew his name, but everyone said he was "the son of a lord," and certainly from his style and bearing he might be the son of almost anything that was high enough in rank. He drew "a remittance," but, as that was paid through Ashley, no one knew from where it came or how much it was. He was a perfect picture of a man, and in all Western skills he was easily first. He could rope a steer, bunch cattle, play poker, or drink whisky to the admiration of his friends and the confusion of his foes, of whom he had a few;

while as to "bronco busting," the skill *par excellence* of western cattlemen, even Bronco Bill was heard to acknowledge that he "wasn't in it with the Duke," for it was his opinion that the Duke could ride anything that had legs under it, even if it were a centipede. And this, coming from one who made a profession of bronco busting, was unquestionably high praise.

The Duke lived alone, except when he deigned to pay a visit to some lonely rancher who, for the marvelous charm of his talk, was delighted to have him as a guest, even at the expense of the loss of a few poker hands. He made a friend of no one, though some men could tell of times when he stood between them and their last dollar, exacting only the promise that no mention should be made of his deed. He had an easy, lazy manner and a slow, cynical smile that rarely left his face, and the only sign of deepening passion in him was a little broadening of his smile.

Old Latour, who kept the Stopping Place, told me about an occasion when he witnessed the Duke actually laughing. A French half-breed freight driver on his way north had entered into a game of poker with the Duke, with the result that his six-months' pay stood in a little heap at his enemy's left hand. The enraged freighter accused his smiling opponent of being a cheat and was proceeding to demolish him with one mighty blow. But the Duke, still smiling, and without moving from his chair, caught the descending fist, slowly crushed the fingers open, and steadily drew the Frenchman to his knees, gripping him so cruelly in the meantime that he was forced to cry aloud for mercy. That was when the Duke broke into a light laugh and, touching the kneeling Frenchman on his cheek with his fingertips, said: "Look here, my man, you shouldn't play the game till you know how to do it and with whom you should play." Then, handing him back the money, he added: "I want money, but not yours." Then, as he sat looking at the unfortunate wretch dividing his attention between his money and his bleeding fingers, he once more broke into a slight laugh that was not good to hear.

The Duke was by all odds the most striking figure in the Company of the Noble Seven, and his word went further than that of any other. His shadow was Bruce, an Edinburgh University man, esoteric, argumentative, persistent, devoted to the Duke. Indeed, his chief ambition was to attain to the Duke's high and lordly manner; but, inasmuch as he was rather squat in figure and had an open, good-natured face and a Scotch voice of the hard and rasping kind, his attempts at imitation were not conspicuously successful.

Every mail that reached Swan Creek brought Bruce a letter from home. At first, after I had gotten to know him, he would occasionally give me a letter to read, but as the tone became more and more anxious he ceased to let me read them, and I was glad enough of this. How he could read those letters and go the pace of the Noble Seven I could not see. Poor Bruce! He had good impulses, a generous heart, but the "Permit" nights and the hunts and the "roundups" and the poker and all the wild excesses of the Company were more that he could stand.

Then there were the two Hill brothers, the younger, Bertie, a fair-haired, bright-faced youngster, none too able to look after himself, but much inclined to follies of all degrees and sorts. He was warm-hearted and devoted to his big brother, Humphrey, called "Hump," who had taken to ranching mainly with the idea of looking after his younger brother. And that was no easy matter, for everyone liked the lad and in consequence let him join in their mischief.

In addition to these there were two others of the original seven, but by force of circumstances they were prevented from any more than a nominal connection with the Company. Blake, a wild Irishman, had joined the police at the Fort, and Gifford had gotten married and, as Bill said, "was roped tighter'n a steer."

The Noble Company, with the cowboys that helped on the range and two or three farmers that lived nearer the Fort, composed the settlers of the Swan Creek country. A strange medley of people of all ranks and nations, but among them there were the evil-hearted and evil-living; however, for the Noble Company I will say that never have I fallen in with men braver, truer, or of warmer heart. Vices they had, all too apparent and deadly, but they were due rather to the circumstances of their lives than to the native tendencies of their hearts. Throughout that summer and the winter following I lived among them, camping on the range with them and sleeping in their shacks, bunching cattle in summer and hunting wolves in winter. Also, being no wiser than they, did I refuse my part on "Permit" nights; but through all, not a man of them ever failed in his friendship and brotherhood.

3

The Coming of the Pilot

He was the first missionary ever seen in the country, and it was the Old Timer who named him. The Old Timer's arrival to the Foothill country was prehistoric, and his influence was, in consequence, immense. None ventured to disagree with him, for to disagree with the Old Timer was to label yourself a tenderfoot, which no one, of course cared to do. To be a newcomer was a misfortune that only time could repair, and it was every newcomer's aim to assume with all possible speed the style and customs of the aristocratic Old Timers, and to forget as soon as possible the date of his own arrival.

I had become schoolmaster of Swan Creek. For in the spring a kind Providence sent in the Muirs and the Bremans with housefuls of children, to the ranchers' disgust, for they foresaw plowed fields and barbed-wire fences cramping their unlimited ranges. A school became necessary. A little log building was erected, and I was appointed schoolmaster.

It was as schoolmaster that I first came to know of the Sky Pilot, who became known simply as "the Pilot." The letter that the Hudson's Bay freighters brought me early one summer evening bore the inscription:

> The Schoolmaster
> Public School
> Swan Creek, Alberta

There was a certain quality about the letter; the writing was in a precise, small hand, and there was something fine in the signature: "Arthur Wellington Moore." He was glad to know that there was a school and a teacher in Swan Creek, for a school meant children, in whom his soul delighted; and in the teacher he would find a friend, and without a friend he could not live. He took me into his confidence, telling me that though he had volunteered for this faraway mission field, he was not at all sure that he would succeed. But he meant to try, and he was charmed at the prospect of having one sympathizer at least. Would I be kind enough to put up in some conspicuous place the enclosed notice, filling in the blanks as I thought best?

> Divine service will be held a week
> from Sunday at Swan Creek
> in _____ _____ at ____ o'clock.
> All are cordially invited.
>
> Arthur Wellington Moore

On the whole I liked his letter. I liked its modest self-depreciation and its cool assumption of my sympathy and cooperation. But I was perplexed. I remembered that Sunday was the day fixed for the great baseball match, when those from "Home," as they fondly called the land across the sea from which they had come, were to "wipe the earth" with all comers. Besides, "divine service" was an innovation in Swan Creek, and I felt sure that, like all innovations that suggested the approach of the East, it would not be welcome.

However, immediately under the notice of the "Grand Baseball Match a week from Sunday, at 2:30, Home vs. the World," I pinned on the door of the Stopping Place the announcement:

> Divine service will be held at Swan Creek, in the Stopping Place parlor, a week from Sunday, immediately upon the conclusion of the baseball match.
> Arthur Wellington Moore

There was a strange incongruity in the two, and an unconscious challenge as well.

All the next day, which was Saturday, and during the following week, I stood guard over my notice, enjoying the excitement it produced and the comments it called forth. It was the advance wave of the great ocean of civilization, which many of them had been glad to leave behind— some wished forever.

To Robert Muir, one of the farmers newly arrived, the notice was a harbinger of good. It stood for progress, markets, and a higher price for land; albeit, he wondered aloud, "hoo he wad be keepit up." His hard-wrought, quick-spoken little wife at his elbow "hooted" agreement with his sentiments, but for altogether different reasons. Thinking of her growing lads, she welcomed with unmixed satisfaction the coming of "the meenister." Her satisfaction was shared by all the mothers and most of the fathers in the settlement.

But by the others, and especially by that rollicking crew, the Company of the Noble Seven, the missionary's coming was viewed with varying degrees of animosity. It meant a limitation of freedom in their reckless living. The "Permit" nights would now, to say the least, be subject to criticism; the Sunday wolf hunts and horse races, with their attendant delights, would now be pursued under the eye of the Church, and this would not add to the enjoyment of them.

One great charm of the country, which Bruce, himself the son of an Edinburgh minister, and now secretary of the Noble Seven, described as "letting a fellow do as he pleased," would be gone. None resented more bitterly than he the missionary's intrusion, which he declared to be an attempt "to reimpose upon their freedom the shackles of an antiquated and bigoted conventionality." The rest of the Company, while not taking so decided a stand, were agreed that the establishment of a church institution was an objectionable and impertinent as well as unnecessary proceeding.

Of course, Hi Kendal and his friend Bronco Bill had no opinion one way or the other. The Church could hardly affect them even remotely. A dozen years' stay in Montana had proved with sufficient clearness to them that a church was a luxury of civilization the West might well do without.

Outside the Company of the Noble Seven there was only one whose opinion had value in Swan Creek, and that was the Old Timer. The Company had sought to bring him in by making him an honorary member, but he refused to be drawn from his home far up among the hills, where he lived with his little girl, Gwen, and her old half-breed nurse, Ponka. He seemed to resent the coming of the Church as a personal injury. It represented to him civilization from which he had fled fifteen years ago with his wife and baby girl, and when five years later he laid his wife in the lonely grave that could be seen on the shaded knoll just fronting his cabin door, the last link to his past was broken. From anything that suggested the world beyond the scope of the prairie, he shrank, as one shrinks from a sudden touch upon a wound that has not yet healed.

"I guess I'll have to move back," he said to me gloomily.

"Why?" I said in surprise, thinking of his grazing range, which was ample for his herd.

"That Sky Pilot." He then swore, and he never swore except when unusually moved.

"Sky Pilot?" I inquired.

He nodded and silently pointed to the notice.

"Oh, well, he won't hurt you, will he?"

"Can't stand it," he answered savagely, "must get away."

"What about Gwen?" I ventured, for she was the light of his eyes. "Pity to stop her studies." I was giving her weekly lessons at the old man's ranch.

"Dunno. Ain't figgered out yet about that baby." She was still his baby.

"Guess she's got all she wants in the Foothills, anyway. What's the use?" he added, talking to himself, as men who spend most of their time alone tend to do.

I waited for a moment, then said: "Well, I wouldn't hurry about doing anything," knowing well that the one thing an Old Timer hates to do is to make any change in his mode of life. "Maybe he won't stay."

He caught at this eagerly. "That's so! There ain't much to keep him, anyway," and he rode off toward his lonely ranch far up in the hills.

I looked after the swaying figure and tried to picture his past with its tragedy; then I found myself wondering how he would end and what would become of his little girl. And I made up my mind that if the missionary were the right sort, his coming might not be a bad thing for the Old Timer and perhaps for more than him.

4

The Pilot's Measure

It was Hi Kendal who announced the arrival of the missionary. I was standing at the door of my school, watching the children ride off on their ponies, when Hi came loping along on his bronco in the loose-jointed cowboy style.

"Well," he drawled out, bringing his bronco to a dead stop in a single bound, "he's lit."

"Lit? Where? What?" said I, looking round for an eagle or some other flying thing.

"Your beloved Sky Pilot, and he's a beauty, a pretty kid—looks too tender for this climate. Better not let him out on the range." Hi swore. He was evidently quite disgusted.

"What's the matter with him, Hi?"

"Why *he* ain't no parson! I don't go much on parsons, but when I calls for one I don't want no bantam chicken. No sirree. I don't want no pink-and-white complected nursery kid foolin' round my graveyard. If you're gonna bring along a parson, why, bring him with his eyeteeth cut and his tail feathers on." Hi swore again.

That Hi was deeply disappointed was quite clear from the selection of the profanity with which he adorned this lengthy address. It was never the extent of his profanity but the choice that indicated Hi's interest in any subject.

Altogether, the outlook for the missionary was not encouraging. With the single exception of the Muirs, who really counted for little, nobody wanted him. To most of the reckless young bloods of the Company of the Noble Seven, his presence was an offense; to others simply a nuisance, while the Old Timer regarded his advent with something like dismay. And now Hi's impression of his personal appearance was not cheering.

My first sight of him did not reassure me. He

was very slight, very young, very innocent, with a face that might do for an angel, except for the touch of humor in it, but which seemed strangely out of place among the rough, hard faces that were to be seen in the Swan Creek country. It was not a weak face, however. The forehead was high and square, the mouth firm, and the eyes were luminous, of some dark color—violet, if there is such a color in eyes—dreamy or sparkling, according to his mood; eyes for which a woman might find use, but which, in a missionary's head, appeared to me one of those extraordinary wastes of which nature is sometimes guilty.

He was gazing far away into space infinitely beyond the Foothills and the blue line of the mountains behind them. He turned to me with eyes alight and face glowing as I drew near.

"It is glorious," he almost panted. "You see this every day?" Then, recalling himself, he came eagerly toward me, stretching out his hand. "You are the schoolmaster, I know. Do you know, it's a great thing? I wanted to be one, but I never could get the boys on. They always got me telling them tales. I was awfully disappointed. I am trying the next best thing. You see, I won't have to keep order. I must admit, though, that I don't think I can preach very well either. I am going to visit your school. Have you many scholars? Do you know, I think it's splendid? I wish I could do it."

I had intended to be somewhat stiff with him, but his evident admiration of me made me quite forget this intention. As he talked on without waiting for an answer, his enthusiasm, his deference to my opinion, and his charming manner made him perfectly irresistible; and before I was aware, I was listening to his plans for working his mission with eager interest. So eager was my interest, that before I was aware, I found myself asking him to tea with me in my shack. But he declined, saying, "I'd like to, awfully, but do you know, I think Latour expects me."

This consideration of Latour's feelings almost upset me.

"You come with me," he added, and I went.

Latour welcomed us with his grim old face wreathed in unusual smiles. The Pilot had been talking to him too.

"I've got it, Latour!" he cried out as he entered. "Here you are," and he broke into the beautiful French-Canadian song, "A' la Claire Fontaine," to the old half-breed's almost tearful delight.

"Do you know," he went on, "I heard that first down the Mattawa," and away he went into a story of an experience with French-Canadian raftsmen, mixing up his French and English in so charming a manner that Latour, who in his younger days long ago had been a shantyman himself, hardly knew whether he was standing on his head or on his heels.

After tea I proposed a ride out to see the sunset from the nearest rising ground. Latour, with unexampled generosity, offered his own cayuse, Louis.

"I can't ride well," protested the Pilot.

"Ah! dat's good ponee, Louis," urged Latour. "He's quiet lak wan little mouse; he's ride lak—what you cal?—wan horse-on-de-rock." Under which persuasion the pony was accepted.

That evening I saw the Swan Creek country with new eyes—through the luminous eyes of the Pilot. We rode up the trail by the side of the Swan till we came to the canyon mouth, dark and full of mystery.

"Come on," I said, "we must get to the top for the sunset."

He looked lingeringly into the deep shadows and asked: "Anything live down there?"

"Coyotes and wolves and ghosts."

"Ghosts?" he asked delightedly. "Do you know, I was sure there were, and I'm quite sure I shall see them."

Then we took Porcupine Trail and climbed for about two miles the gentle slope to the top of the first rising ground. There we stayed and watched the sun take its nightly plunge into the sea of mountains, now dimly visible. Behind us stretched the prairie, sweeping out level to the sky and cut by the winding canyon of the Swan. Before us lay the hills and far beyond them, up against the sky, was the line of mountains—blue, purple, and gold, according to the light that fell on them. We stood long without a word or movement, filling our hearts with the silence and the beauty, till the gold in the west began to grow dim. High above all, the night was stretching her star-pierced canopy, and the great silence of the dying day had fallen upon the world and held us fast.

"Listen," he said, pointing to the hills. "Can't you hear them breathe?"

And, looking at their curving shoulders, I fancied I could see them slowly heaving as if in heavy sleep, and I was quite sure I could hear them breathe. I was under the spell of the Sky Pilot's voice and eyes, and all of nature was completely alive to me.

We rode back to the Stopping Place in silence, except for a word of mine now and then that he didn't acknowledge, and, with hardly a good night, he left me at the door. I turned away feeling as if I had been in a strange country and among strange people.

How would he do with Swan Creek folk? Could he make them see the hills breathe? Would they feel as I felt under his voice and eyes? What a curious mixture he was. I was doubtful about his first Sunday, and I was surprised to find all my indifference as to his success or failure gone. It was a pity about the baseball game. I would speak to some of the men about it tomorrow.

Hi might be disappointed in his appearance, but, as I turned into my shack and thought over my last two hours with the Pilot and how he had "gotten to" old Latour and myself, I began to think that Hi might be mistaken in his measure of the Pilot.

5

First Blood

One is never enthusiastic in the early morning for impossible tasks, but they are easier when faced straight on. I was determined to try to have the baseball game postponed. There could be no difficulty. One day was as much of a holiday as another to these easygoing fellows.

But the Duke, when I suggested the change for this day, simply raised his eyebrows an eighth of an inch and said, "Can't see why the day should be changed."

The others followed the Duke's lead. Bruce

stormed and swore all kinds of destruction upon himself if he was going to change his style of life for any man.

That Sunday was a day of incongruities. The Old and the New, the East and the West, the reverential Past and iconoclastic Present were scrambling themselves together in bewildering confusion. The baseball game was played with much vigor and profanity.

The expression on the Pilot's face, as he stood watching, was a curious mixture of interest, surprise, doubt, and pain. He was readjusting himself to this new situation and so was extremely sensitive to his surroundings. The color of his face told of the level of discomfort he felt. Discomfort by the indifference and blatant disregard to all he held sacred and essential. They were all so dead sure. How did he know they were wrong? It was his first close view of practical, living skepticism. Skepticism in a book did not disturb him; he could put down words against it. But here it was alive, cheerful, and fascinating, for these Western men with their garb and habits had captured his imagination. He was in a fierce struggle, and in a few minutes I saw him disappear into the canyon.

Meantime the game went uproariously on to a finish, with the result that the champions of "Home" had "to stand The Painkiller," their defeat being due chiefly to the work of Bronco Bill and Hi as pitcher and catcher.

The celebration was in full swing, or as Hi put it, "the boys were takin' their pizen good an' calm," when in walked the Pilot. His face was still troubled and his lips were drawn and blue, as if he were in pain. He stood a moment hesitating, looking on the faces flushed and hot and now turned toward him in curious defiance. He noticed the look, and it pulled him together. He turned to old Latour and asked in a high, clear voice:

"Is this the room you said we might have?"

The Frenchman shrugged and said, "There is not any more."

The Pilot paused for an instant, but only for an instant. Then, lifting a pile of hymnbooks he had near him on the bar, he said in a grave, sweet voice, and with the quiver of a smile about his lips, "Gentlemen, Mr. Latour has allowed me this room for a religious service. It will give me great pleasure if you will all join."

The Pilot handed a book to Bronco Bill, who,

surprised, took it as if he did not know what to do with it. The others followed Bronco's lead till he came to Bruce, who refused, saying roughly, "No! I don't want it; I've no use for it."

The missionary flushed and drew back as if he had been struck, but immediately, as if unconsciously, the Duke, who was standing near, stretched out his hand and said, with a courteous bow, "I thank you. I should be glad of one."

"Thank you," replied the Pilot as he handed him a book. The men seated themselves on the bench that ran round the room, or they just leaned up against the bar, and most of them took off their hats. Just then in came Muir, and behind him his little wife. In an instant the Duke was on his feet, and every hat came off.

The missionary stood up at the bar and announced the hymn, "Jesus, Lover of My Soul." The silence that followed was broken by the sound of a horse galloping. A buckskin bronco shot past the window, and in a few moments there appeared at the door the Old Timer. He was about to stride in when the unusual sight of a row of men sitting solemnly with hymnbooks in their hands held him fast at the door. He gazed in an amazed, helpless way upon the men, then at the missionary, then back at the men, and stood speechless. Suddenly there was a high, shrill, boyish laugh, and the men turned to see the missionary in a fit of laughter. It certainly was a shock to any lingering ideas of religious propriety they might have about them, but the contrast between his frank, laughing face and the amazed and disgusted look of the shaggy old man in the doorway was too much for them, and one by one they gave way to roars of laughter. The Old Timer, however, kept his face unmoved, strode up to the bar, and nodded to old Latour, who served him his drink, which he took at a gulp.

"Here, old man!" called out Bill, "get into the game; here's your deck," offering him his book. But the missionary was before him, and, with very beautiful grace, he handed the Old Timer a book and pointed him to a seat.

I shall never forget that service. As a religious affair, it was a dead failure, but somehow I think the Pilot, as Hi approvingly said, "got in his funny work," and it was not wholly a defeat. The first hymn was sung chiefly by the missionary and Mrs. Muir, whose voice was very high, with one or two men softly whistling an accompaniment.

The second hymn was better, and then came the lesson, the story of the feeding of the five thousand. As the missionary finished the story, Bill, who had been listening with great interest, said, "I say, pard, I think I'll call you just now."

"I beg your pardon!" said the startled missionary.

"You're givin' us quite a song and dance now, ain't you?"

"I don't understand," was the puzzled reply.

"How many men was there in that crowd?" asked Bill, with a judicial air.

"Five thousand."

"And how much grub?"

"Five loaves and two fishes," answered Bruce for the missionary.

"Well," drawled Bill, with the air of a man who has reached a conclusion, "that's a little too unusual for me. Why," looking pityingly at the missionary, "it ain't natural."

"Not for Him," said the missionary. Then Bruce joyfully took him up and led him on into a discussion of evidences, and from evidences into metaphysics, the origin of evil and the freedom of the will, until the missionary, as Bill said, "was rattled worse than a rooster in the dark."

Poor Mrs. Muir was much scandalized and looked anxiously at her husband, wishing him to take her out. But help came from an unexpected quarter, and Hi suddenly called out, "Here you, Bill, shut your jaw, and you, Bruce, give the man a chance to work off his music."

"That's so! Play fair! Go on!" were the cries that came in response to Hi's appeal.

The missionary, who was all trembling and much troubled, gave Hi a grateful look, and said:

"I'm afraid there are a great many things I don't understand, and I am not good at argument."

There were shouts of "Go on! Fire ahead; play the game!" but he said, "I think we will close the service with a hymn." His frankness and modesty and his respectful, courteous manner gained the sympathy of the men, so that all joined heartily in singing "Sun of My Soul." In the prayer that followed, his voice grew steady and his nerve came back to him. The words were very simple, and the petitions were mostly for light and for strength. With a few words of remembrance of "those in our homes far away who think of us and pray for us and never forget," this strange service was brought to a close.

After the missionary had stepped out, the whole affair was discussed with great intensity. Hi Kendal said "The Pilot didn't have no fair show," maintaining that when he was "ropin' a steer he didn't want no tenderfoot to be shovin' in his rope like Bill there."

But Bill steadily maintained his position that "the story of that there picnic was a little too unusual" for him. Bruce was trying meanwhile to beguile the Duke into a discussion of the metaphysics of the case. But the Duke refused with quiet contempt to be drawn into a region where he felt himself a stranger. He preferred poker himself, if Bruce cared to take a hand. And so the evening went on, with the theological discussion by Hi and Bill in a friendly spirit in one corner, while the others for the most part played poker.

When the missionary returned later, there were only a few left in the room, among them the Duke and Bruce, who was drinking steadily and losing money. The missionary's presence seemed to irritate Bruce, and he played even more recklessly than usual, swearing deeply at every loss.

At the door the missionary stood looking up

into the night sky and humming softly "Sun of My Soul," and after a few minutes the Duke joined in humming bass to the air till Bruce could contain himself no longer.

"I say," he called out, "this isn't any prayer meeting, is it?" He then swore.

The Duke ceased humming, and, looking at Bruce, said quietly, "Well, what is it? What's the trouble?"

"Trouble!" shouted Bruce. "I don't see what hymn singing has to do with a poker game."

"Oh, I see! I beg pardon! Was I singing?" said the Duke. Then after a pause he added, "You're quite right. I say, Bruce, let's quit. Something has gotten on your nerves." And coolly sweeping his pile into his pocket, he gave up the game. With an oath Bruce left the table, took another drink, and went unsteadily out to his horse, and soon we heard him ride away into the darkness, singing snatches of the hymn and swearing the most awful oaths.

The missionary's face was white with horror. It was all new and terrible to him.

"Will he get safely home?" he asked of the Duke.

"Don't you worry, youngster," said the Duke in his loftiest manner, "he'll get along."

The luminous, dreamy eyes grew hard and bright as they looked the Duke in the face.

"Yes, I shall worry; but you ought to worry more."

"Ah!" said the Duke, raising his brows and smiling gently upon the bright, stern, young face lifted up to his. "I didn't notice that I had asked your opinion."

"If anything should happen to him," replied the missionary, quickly, "I should consider you largely responsible."

"That would be kind," said the Duke, still smiling with his lips. But after a moment's steady look into the missionary's eyes he nodded his head twice and without further word, turned away.

The missionary turned eagerly to me:

"They beat me this afternoon," he cried, "but thank God, I know now they are wrong and I am right! I don't understand. I can't see my way through. But I am right! It's true! I feel it's true! Men can't live without Him and be men!"

And long after I went to my shack that night, I saw before me the eager face with the luminous eyes and heard the triumphant cry: "I feel it's true! Men can't live without Him and be men!" And I knew that though his first Sunday ended in defeat, there was victory yet awaiting him.

6

His Second Wind

The first weeks were not pleasant for the Pilot. He had been beaten, and the sense of failure dampened his enthusiasm, which was one of his chief charms. The Noble Seven despised, ignored, or laughed at him according to their mood and disposition. Bruce patronized him, and, worst of all, the Muirs pitied him. It was the Muirs' pity that brought him low, and I was glad of it. I find it hard to put up with a man that enjoys pity.

It was Hi Kendal that restored him, though

Hi had no thought of doing so good a deed. It happened in this way: A baseball match was on with the Porcupines from near the Fort. To Hi's disgust and the team's dismay, Bill failed to appear. It was Hi's job to catch Bill's pitching, and together their batting was the glory of the Home team.

"Try the Pilot, Hi," said someone, goading him.

Hi looked glumly across at the Pilot standing some distance away, then called out, holding up the ball, "Can you play the game?"

As a reply, Moore held up his hands for a catch. Hi lobbed the ball to him. The ball came back so quickly that Hi was hardly ready, and the force of the throw seemed to amaze him.

"I'll take him," he said doubtfully, and the game began. Hi proudly put on his mask, a new device, and waited.

"How do you like them?" asked the Pilot.

"Hot!" said Hi. "I hain't got no gloves to burn."

The Pilot turned his back, swung off one foot on to the other, and rocketed the ball past the batter.

"Strike!" called the umpire.

"You bet!" said Hi, with emphasis, but his face was a picture of amazement and dawning delight.

Again the Pilot went through the maneuver on the mound, and again the umpire called "Strike!"

Hi stopped the ball without holding it and set himself for the third. Once more that disconcerting swing and the whiplike action of the arm, and for the third time the umpire called "Strike! Striker out!"

"That's the hole!" yelled Hi.

The Porcupines were amazed. Hi looked at the ball in his hand, then at the slight figure of the Pilot.

"I say! Where do you get it?"

"What?" Moore innocently asked.

"The gait!"

"The what?"

"The gait! The speed, you know!"

"Oh! I used to play for Princeton a little."

"Did, eh? What did you quit for?"

He evidently regarded the exchange of the profession of baseball for the study of theology as a serious error in judgment, and every inning of the game confirmed his opinion. At bat the Pilot did not shine, but he made up for light hitting by his baserunning. He was fleet as a deer, and he knew the game thoroughly. He was keen, eager, intense in play, and before the innings were half over, he was recognized as the best all-around man on the field. On the pitcher's mound he puzzled the Porcupines till they grew desperate and hit wildly and blindly, amid the jeers of the spectators. The bewilderment of the Porcupines was equaled only by the enthusiasm of Hi and his team, and when the game was over the score stood 37 to 7 in favor of the Home team. They carried the Pilot off the field.

From that day Moore was another man. He had won the unqualified respect of Hi Kendal and most of the others, for he could beat them at their own game and still be modest about it. Once more his enthusiasm came back along with his brightness and courage. The Duke was not present to witness his triumph, and, besides, he rather despised the game. Bruce was there, however, but took no part in the general acclaim; indeed, he seemed rather disgusted with Moore's sudden leap into favor. Certainly his hostility to the Pilot and all that he stood for was none the less open and bitter.

Bruce's hostility was more than usually marked at the service held on the following Sunday. It was, perhaps, thrown into a greater contrast by the open and delighted approval of Hi, who was prepared to back up anything the Pilot would venture to say. Bill, who had not witnessed the Pilot's performance in the game, but had only Hi's enthusiastic report to go upon, still preserved his judicial air. It is fair to say that there was no mean-spirited jealousy in Bill's heart even though Hi had frankly assured him that the Pilot was "a demon of a pitcher" and could "give him points."

Bill had great confidence in Hi's opinion about baseball, but he was not prepared to surrender his right of private judgment in matters theological, so he waited for the sermon before committing himself or venturing any approval. This service was an undoubted success. The singing was hearty, and unconsciously the men fell into a reverent attitude during prayer. The theme, too, was one that gave little room for skepticism.

It was the story of Zaccheus, and storytelling was Moore's strong point. The thing was well done. Vivid portrayals of the outcast, shrewd, converted publican and the supercilious, self-complacent, critical Pharisee were drawn with a few deft touches. A single sentence transferred them to the Foothills and arrayed them in cowboy garb. Bill was none too sure of himself, but Hi, with delightful winks, was indicating Bruce as the Pharisee, to the latter's scornful disgust. The preacher must have noticed, for with a very clever turn the Pharisee was shown to be the kind of man who likes to fit faults upon others. Bill, digging his elbows into Hi's ribs, said in an audible whisper, "Say, pardner, how does it fit now?"

"You git out!" answered Hi, but his confidence in his interpretation of the application was shaken. When Moore came to describe the Master and His place in that ancient group, we in the Stopping Place parlor fell under the spell of his eyes and voice, and our hearts were moved. That great Personality was made very real and very winning. Hi was quite subdued by the story and the picture. Bill was perplexed; it was all new to him. Bruce was mainly irritated. To him it was all old and filled with memories he hated to face. At any rate, he was unusually savage that evening, drank heavily, and went home late, raging and cursing at things in general and the Pilot in particular—for Moore, in a timid sort of way, had tried to quiet him and help him to his horse.

"Ornery sort o' beast now, ain't he?" said Hi, with the idea of comforting the Pilot who stood sadly looking after Bruce disappearing into the gloom.

"No! no!" he answered, "not a beast, but a brother."

"Brother! Not much, if I know my relations!" answered Hi, disgustedly.

"The Master thinks a good deal of him," was the earnest reply.

"Git out!" said Hi. "You don't mean it! Why, he's more stuck on himself than that mean old cuss you was tellin' about this afternoon, and without half the reason."

But Moore only said, "Don't be too hard on him, Hi," and turned away, leaving Hi and Bill gravely discussing the question, with the aid of several drinks of whisky. They were still discussing when, an hour later, they too disappeared into the darkness that swallowed up the trail to Ashley Ranch.

That was the first of many such services. The preaching was always of the simplest kind, abstract questions being avoided, and the concrete in those wonderful Bible tales, dressed in modern, western garb, set forth. Bill and Hi were more than ever his friends and champions, and the latter was heard exultantly to exclaim to Bruce, "He ain't much to look at as a parson, but he's a ketchin' his second wind, and 'fore long you won't see him for dust."

7

The Last of the Permit Sundays

The spring roundups were all over and Bruce had nothing to do but loaf about the Stopping Place, drinking old Latour's bad whisky and making himself a nuisance. In vain the Pilot tried to win him with loans of books and magazines and other kindly courtesies. Bruce would be decent for a day and then would break out with violent arguments against religion and all who held to it. He sorely missed the Duke, who had gone south on one of his periodic journeys. The Duke's presence always steadied Bruce and took the rasp out of his behavior. It was rather a relief to all that he was absent from the next fortnightly service, though Moore declared he was ashamed to admit it.

"I can't touch him," Moore said to me after the service. "He is far too clever, but," and his voice was full of pain, "I'd give anything to help him."

"If he doesn't quit his nonsense," I replied, "he'll soon be past helping. He doesn't go out on his range, his few cattle wander everywhere, his shack is in a beastly state, and he himself is going to pieces." For it did seem a shame that a fellow should so throw himself away for nothing.

"You are hard," said Moore, with his eyes upon me.

"Hard? Isn't it true?" I answered hotly. "Then, there's his mother at home."

"Yes, but can he help it? Is it all his fault?" he replied, with his steady eyes looking into me.

"His fault? Whose fault then?"

"What of the Noble Seven? Have they anything to do with this?" His voice was quiet, but there was an arresting intensity in it.

"Well," I said, rather weakly, "a man ought to look after himself."

"Yes—and his brother a little." Then he added, "What have any of you done to help him? The Duke could have pulled him up a year ago if he had been willing to deny himself a little, and so with all of you. You all do just what pleases you regardless of any other, and so you help one another down."

I could not find anything just then to say, though afterwards many things came to me; for, though his voice was quiet and low, his eyes were glowing and his face was alight with the fire that burned within, and I felt like one convicted of a crime. This was certainly a new doctrine for the West—an uncomfortable doctrine to practice, interfering seriously with personal liberty, but in the Pilot's way of viewing things, difficult to escape. There would be no end to one's responsibility. I refused to think it out.

Within a week we were thinking it out with some intentness. The Noble Seven were to have a great "blowout" at the Hill brothers' ranch. The Duke had returned home from his southern trip a little more weary looking and a little more cynical in his smile. The blowout was to be held on Permit Sunday, the alternate to the Preaching Sunday. This was a concession to the Pilot, secured mainly through the influence of Hi and his baseball nine. It was a notable accomplishment to have created the distinction between Preaching and Permit Sundays. Hi put it rather graphically: "The devil takes his innin's one Sunday and the Pilot the next," adding emphatically, "He hain't done much scorin' yit, but my money's on the Pilot!" Bill was more cautious and preferred to wait for developments. And developments were rapid.

The Hill brothers' gathering was unusually successful from a social point of view. Several Permits had been requisitioned, and whisky and beer abounded. Races all day and poker all night, with varying impromptu diversions—such as shooting the horns off wandering steers—were the social activities indulged in by the noble company. On Monday evening I rode out to the ranch, urged by Moore, who was anxious that someone should look after Bruce.

"I don't belong to them," he said. "You do. They won't resent your coming."

Nor did they. They were sitting at supper, and welcomed me with a shout.

"Hello, old dominie!" yelled Bruce, "where's your preacher friend?"

"Where you ought to be, if you could get there—at home," I replied, nettled at his insolent tone.

"Strike one!" called out Hi, enthusiastically, not approving Bruce's attitude toward his friend, the Pilot.

"Don't be so acute," said Bruce, after the laughter had passed, "but have a drink."

He was flushed and very shaky and very noisy. The Duke, at the head of the table, looked a little harder than usual, but, though pale, was quite steady. About the room were the signs of a wild night. A bench was upset, while broken bottles and crockery lay strewn about over a floor reeking with filth. The disgust on my face brought an apology from the younger Hill, who was serving up ham and eggs as best he could to the men lounging about the table.

"It's my housemaid's afternoon out," he explained gravely.

"Gone for a walk in the park," added another.

"Hope the schoolmaster will pardon the absence," sneered Bruce, in his most offensive manner.

"Don't mind him," said Hi, under his breath, "the blue devils are runnin' him down."

This became more evident as the evening went on. From hilarity Bruce passed to sullen ferocity, with spasms of nervous terror. Hi's attempts to soothe him finally drove him mad, and he drew his revolver, declaring he could look after himself, and to prove it he began shooting out the lights.

The men scrambled into safe corners, all but the Duke, who stood quietly watching Bruce. Then saying, "Let me have a try, Bruce," he reached across and caught his hand.

"No! you don't," said Bruce, struggling. "No man gets my gun."

He tore madly at the gripping hand with both of his, but in vain, calling out with rightful oaths, "Let go! Let go! I'll kill you! I'll kill you!"

With a furious effort he hurled himself back from the table, dragging the Duke partly across. There was a shot and Bruce collapsed, the Duke still gripping him. When he lifted him he was found to have an ugly wound in his arm, the bullet having passed through the fleshy part. I bound it up as best I could and tried to persuade him to go to bed. But he was determined to go home. Nothing could stop him. Finally the Duke agreed to go with him, and off they set, Bruce loudly protesting that he could get home alone and did not want anyone.

It was a dismal breakup to the affair, and we all went home feeling rather sick, so that it gave me no pleasure to find Moore waiting in my shack for my report of Bruce. It was quite useless for me to make light of the accident to him. His eyes were wide open with anxious fear when I had finished.

"You needn't tell me not to be worried," he said. "You are worried yourself. I see it; I feel it."

"Well, there's no use trying to keep things from you," I replied, "but I am only a little worried. Don't you go and work yourself up into a fever over it."

"Oh, nonsense, it isn't coming to that, but I wish he were in better shape. He is broken up badly enough without this hole in him."

He would not leave till I had promised to take him to see Bruce the next day, though I was doubtful of the reception he would receive. But the next day the Duke came down, his black bronco, Jingo, wet with hard riding.

"Better come up, Connor," he said gravely, "and bring your bromides along. He has had a bad night and morning and fell asleep just before

I left. I expect he'll wake in delirium. It's the whisky more than the bullet. Snakes, you know."

In ten minutes we three were on the trail, for Moore, though not invited, quietly announced his intention to go with us.

"Oh, all right," said the Duke. "He probably won't recognize you anyway."

We rode hard for half an hour till we came within sight of Bruce's shack, which was set back into a little poplar bluff.

"Hold up!" said the Duke. "Was that a shot?" We stood listening. A rifle shot rang out, and we rode hard. Again the Duke halted us, and there came from the shack the sound of singing. It was an old Scotch tune.

"The twenty-third Psalm," Moore whispered.

We rode into the bluff, tied up our horses, and crept to the back of the shack. Looking through a crack between the logs, I saw a gruesome thing. Bruce was sitting up in bed with a Winchester rifle across his knees and a belt of cartridges hanging over the post. His bandages were torn off, the blood from his wound was smeared over his bare arms and his pale, ghastly face, his eyes were wild with mad terror, and he was shouting at the top of his voice, "The Lord's my shepherd;

I'll not want. He makes me down to lie. In pastures green, He leadeth me the quiet waters by."

Now and then he would stop to say in an eerie whisper, "Come out here, you little devils!" and bang would go his rifle at the stovepipe, which was riddled with holes. Then once more in a loud voice he would hurry to begin the Psalm, "The Lord's my Shepherd . . ."

Nothing that my memory brings to me makes me chill like that picture—the low log shack, now in cheerless disorder; the ghastly object upon the bed in the corner, with blood-smeared face and arms and mad terror in the eyes; the awful cursings and more awful psalm singing, punctuated by the quick report of the deadly rifle.

For some moments we stood gazing at one another; then the Duke said in a low, fierce tone, more to himself than to us, "This is the last. There'll be no more of this cursed folly among the boys."

And I thought it a wise thing that the Pilot didn't say a word.

8

The Pilot's Grip

The situation was one of extreme danger—a madman with a Winchester rifle. Something must be done and quickly. But what? It would be death to anyone appearing at the door.

"I'll speak; you keep your eyes on him," said the Duke.

"Hello, Bruce! What's the row?" shouted the Duke.

Instantly the singing stopped. A look of cunning delight came over his face as, without a word, he got his rifle ready and pointed it at the door.

"Come in!" he yelled, after waiting for some moments. "Come in! You're the biggest of all the devils. Come on, I'll send you down where you belong. Come, what's keeping you?"

"I don't relish a bullet much," I said.

"There are pleasanter things," responded the Duke, "and he is a fairly good shot."

Meantime the singing had started again, and, looking through the chink, I saw that Bruce had his eye on the stovepipe again. While I was looking the Pilot slipped away from us toward the door.

"Come back!" said the Duke, "don't be a fool! Come back, he'll shoot you dead!"

Moore paid no attention to him, but stood waiting at the door. In a few moments Bruce blazed away again at the stovepipe. Immediately the Pilot burst in, calling out eagerly, "Did you get him?"

"No!" said Bruce. "He dodged like the devil."

"I'll get him," said Moore. "Smoke him out," proceeding to open the stove door.

"Stop!" screamed Bruce. "Don't open that door! It's full, I tell you." Moore paused. "Besides," went on Bruce, "smoke won't touch 'em."

"Oh, that's all right," said Moore, coolly and with admirable quickness, "wood smoke, you know—they can't stand that."

This was apparently a new idea in demonology for Bruce, for he sank back, while Moore lighted the fire and put on the tea kettle. He looked around for the tea caddy.

"Up there," said Bruce, forgetting for the moment his devils and pointing to a quaint, old-fashioned tea caddy up on the shelf.

"Old country, eh?"

"My mother's," said Bruce, soberly.

"I could have sworn it was my aunt's in Balleymena," said Moore. "My aunt lived in a little stone cottage with roses all over the front of it." And on he went into an enthusiastic description of his early home. His voice was full of music, soft and soothing, and poor Bruce sank back and listened, the glitter fading from his eyes.

The Duke and I looked at each other.

"Not too bad, eh?" said the Duke, after a few moments' silence.

"Let's put up the horses," I suggested. "They won't want us for half an hour."

When we came in, the room had been set in order, the tea kettle was singing, the bed clothes straightened out, and Moore had just finished washing the blood stains from Bruce's arms and neck.

"Just in time," he said. "I didn't like to tackle these," pointing to the bandages.

All night long Moore soothed and tended the sick man, singing softly to him and again beguiling him with tales that meant nothing. Moore had a strange power to quiet Bruce's nervous restlessness, which was due partly to the pain of the wounded arm and partly to the drinking-induced, wrecked nerves. The Duke seemed uncomfortable. He spoke to Bruce once or twice, but the only answer was a groan or curse with an increase of restlessness.

"He'll have a close squeak," said the Duke. The carelessness of the tone was a little overdone, but the Pilot was stirred up by it.

"He has not been fortunate in his friends," he said, looking straight into his eyes.

"A man ought to know himself when the pace is too swift," said the Duke, a little too quickly.

"You might have done something with him. Why didn't you help him?"

Moore's tones were stern and very steady, and he never turned his eyes from the other man's face, but the only reply he got was a shrug of the shoulders.

When the gray of the morning was coming in at the window, the Duke rose up, gave himself a little shake, and said, "I am not of any service here. I shall come back in the evening."

He went and stood for a few moments looking down upon the hot, fevered face; then, turning to me, he asked, "What do you think?"

"Can't say! The bromide is holding him down now."

"Can I get anything?" I knew him well enough to recognize the anxiety under his indifferent manner.

"The Fort doctor ought to be got."

He nodded and went out.

"Have breakfast?" called out Moore from the door.

"I shall get some at the Fort, thanks. I won't do any hurt there," he said, smiling his cynical smile.

Moore's eyes widened in surprise.

"What's that for?" he asked me.

"Well, he is rather cut up, and you rather rubbed it into him, you know," I said, for I thought Moore a little hard.

"Did I say anything untrue?"

"Well, not untrue, perhaps; but truth is like medicine—not always good to take." At which Moore was silent till his patient needed him again.

It was a weary day. The intense pain from the wound and the high fever from the poison in his blood kept the poor fellow in delirium till evening, when the Duke rode up with the Fort doctor. Jingo appeared as nearly played out as a horse of his spirit ever allowed himself to become.

"Seventy miles," said the Duke, swinging himself off the saddle. "The doctor was ten miles out. How is he?"

I shook my head, and he led away his horse to give him a rub and feed.

Meantime the doctor, who was army and had seen service, was examining his patient. He grew more and more puzzled as he noted the various symptoms. Finally he broke out, "What have you been doing to him? Why is he in this condition? This fleabite doesn't account for all," he said, pointing to the wound.

We stood like children reproved. Hesitatingly, the Duke said, "I fear, doctor, that life has been a little too hard for him. He had a severe nervous attack—seeing things, you know."

"Yes, I know," stormed the old doctor. "I know you well enough, with your head of cast iron and no nerves to speak of. I know the crowd and how you lead them. Infernal fools! You'll get your turn some day. I've warned you before."

The Duke was standing before the doctor during this storm, smiling slightly. All at once the smile faded out and he pointed to the bed. Bruce was sitting up quiet and steady. He stretched out his hand to the Duke.

"Don't mind the old goat," Bruce said, holding the Duke's hand and looking up at him as fondly as if he were a girl. "It's my own funeral. Funeral?" He paused. "Perhaps it may be—who knows? Feels bad enough. But remember, Duke—it's my own fault—don't listen to those fools," he said, looking toward Moore and the doctor. "My own fault"—his voice died down—"my own fault."

The Duke bent over him and laid him back on the pillow, saying, "Thanks, old chap, you're good stuff. I'll not forget. Just keep quiet now and you'll be all right." He passed his cool, firm hand over the hot brow of the man looking up at him with love in his eyes, and in a few moments Bruce fell asleep. Then the Duke lifted himself up, and, facing the doctor, said in his coolest tone, "Your words are more true than opportune, doctor. Your patient will need all your attention. As for my morals, Mr. Moore kindly entrusts himself with the care of them." This with a bow toward the Pilot.

"I wish him joy of his charge," snorted the doctor, turning again to the bed, where Bruce had already passed back into delirium.

The memory of that vigil was like a horrible month-long nightmare. Moore lay on the floor and slept. The Duke rode off somewhere, and the old doctor and I kept watch. All night poor Bruce raved in the wildest raving, singing, now psalms, now songs, swearing at the cattle or his poker partners, and now and then, in quieter moments, he was back in his old home, a boy, with a boy's friends and sports. Nothing could check the fever. It baffled the doctor, who often, during the night, declared that there was "no sense in a wound like that working up such a fever," adding curses upon the folly of the Duke and his company.

"You think he will get better, doctor?" I asked, in answer to one of his outbreaks.

Slowly, deliberately, the doctor answered: "I don't think he'll make it."

Everything stood still for a moment. It seemed impossible. Two days ago full of life, now on the way out. There crowded in upon me thoughts of his home; his mother, whose letters he used to show me full of anxious love; his wild life here, with all its generous impulses, its mistakes, its folly.

"How long will he last?" I asked, and my lips were dry and numb.

"Perhaps twenty-four hours, perhaps longer. He can't throw off the poison."

After another day of agonized delirium Bruce sank into a stupor that lasted through the night.

Then the change came. As the light began to grow at the eastern rim of the prairie and light the mountaintops far in the west, Bruce opened his eyes and looked up at us. The doctor had gone; the Duke had not come back; Moore and I were alone. He gazed at us steadily for some moments, read our faces, and a look of wonder came into his eyes.

"Is it coming?" he asked in a faint, awed voice. "Do you really think I must go?"

The eager appeal in his voice and the wistful longing in the wide-open, startled eyes were too much for Moore. He backed behind me, and I could hear him weeping like a baby. Bruce heard him too.

"Is that the Pilot?" he asked. Instantly Moore pulled himself up, wiped his eyes, and came around to the other side of the bed and looked down, smiling.

"Do *you* say I am dying?" Bruce's voice was strained in its earnestness.

I felt a thrill of admiration go through me as the Pilot answered in a sweet, clear voice: "They say so, Bruce. But you are not afraid?"

Bruce kept his eyes on his face and answered with grave hesitation, "No. Not . . . afraid. But I'd like to live a little longer. I've made such a mess of it; I'd like to try again." Then he paused, and his lips quivered a little. "There's my mother, you know," he added, apologetically "and Jim." Jim was his younger brother and sworn chum.

"Yes, I know, Bruce, but it won't be very long for them too, and it's a good place."

"Yes, I believe it all . . . always did. I talked rot—you'll forgive me that?"

"Don't, don't," said Moore quickly, with sharp pain in his voice.

Bruce smiled a little and closed his eyes, saying, "I'm tired." But he immediately opened them again and looked up.

"What is it?" asked Moore, smiling down into his eyes.

"The Duke," the poor lips whispered.

"He is coming," said Moore, confidently, though how he knew I could not tell. But even as he spoke, I looked out the window and saw Jingo come swinging round the bluff. Bruce heard the beat of his hoofs, smiled, opened his eyes, and waited. The leap of joy in his eyes as the Duke came in, clean, cool, and fresh as the morning, went to my heart.

Neither man said a word, but Bruce took hold of the Duke's hand in both of his. He was fast growing weaker. I gave him brandy, and he recovered a little strength.

"I am dying, Duke," he said, quietly. "Promise you won't blame yourself."

"I can't, old man," said the Duke, with a shudder. "Would to heaven I could."

"You were too strong for me, and you didn't think, did you?" and the weak voice had a caress in it.

"No, no! God knows," the Duke said.

There was a long silence, and again Bruce opened his eyes and whispered, "The Pilot."

Moore came to him.

"Read 'The Prodigal,'" he said faintly. And in Moore's clear, sweet voice the music of that matchless story fell on our ears.

Again Bruce's eyes summoned me. I bent over him.

"My letter," he said faintly, "in my coat . . ."

I brought to him the last letter from his mother. He held the envelope before his eyes, then handed it to me, whispering, "Read."

I opened the letter and looked at the words "My darling Davie." My tongue stuck and I couldn't make a sound. Moore put out his hand and took it from me. The Duke rose to go out, calling me with his eyes, but Bruce motioned him to stay, and he sat down and bowed his head while Moore read the letter.

Moore's tone was clear and steady till he came to the last words, when his voice broke and ended in a sob: *"And oh, Davie, Laddie, if ever your heart turns home again, remember the door is aye open, and it's joy you'll bring with you to us all."*

Bruce lay quite still, and, from his closed eyes, big tears ran down his cheeks. It was his last farewell to her whose love had been to him the anchor to all things pure here and to heaven beyond.

He took the letter from Moore's hand, put it with difficulty to his lips, and then, touching the open Bible, he said between his breaths, "It's . . . very like . . . there's really . . . no fear, is there?"

"No, no!" said Moore, with cheerful, confident voice, though his tears were flowing. "No fear of your welcome."

"What shall I tell her?" I asked, trying to recall him. But the message was never given. He moved one hand slowly toward the Duke till it touched his head. The Duke lifted his face and looked down at him, and then he did a beautiful thing for which I forgave him much. He leaned over and kissed the lips grown so white, and then the brow. The light came back into the eyes of the dying man, he smiled once more, and smilingly faced toward the Great Beyond. And the morning air, fresh from the sun-tipped mountains and sweet with the scent of wild roses, came blowing soft and cool through the open window upon the dead, smiling face.

Again the Duke did a beautiful thing. Reaching across his dead friend, he offered his hand to the Pilot. "Mr. Moore," he said, with fine courtesy, "you are a brave man and a good man. I ask your forgiveness for much rudeness."

But Moore only shook his head while he took the outstretched hand, and said, "Don't! I can't stand it."

"The Company of the Noble Seven will meet no more," said the Duke, with a faint smile.

They did meet, however; but when they did, the Pilot was in the chair, and it was not for poker.

The Pilot had "got his grip," as Bill said.

9

Gwen

It was not many days after my arrival in the Foothill country that I began to hear of Gwen. They all had stories of her. The details were not many, but the impression was vivid. She lived far up in the hills near Devil's Lake, and she never ventured from her father's ranch. But some of the men had had glimpses of her and had come to definite opinions regarding her.

"What is she like?" I asked Bill one day, trying to pin him down to something like a descriptive account of her.

"Like! She's a terror," he said, with slow emphasis, "a holy terror."

"But what is she like? What does she look like?" I asked impatiently.

"Look like?" He considered a moment, looked slowly around as if searching for a simile, then answered, "I dunno."

"Don't know? What do you mean? Haven't you seen her?"

"Yeah! But she ain't nothin'."

Bill was quite decided on this point.

I tried again. "Well what sort of hair has she got? She's got hair I suppose?"

"Hayer! Well, a few!" said Bill, with some choice profanity in response to my suggestion. "Yards of it! Red!"

"Git out!" contradicted Hi. "Red! Tain't no more red than mine!"

Bill regarded Hi's hair critically.

"What color do you put onto your brush?" he asked cautiously.

"Tain't no difference. Tain't red anyhow."

"Red! Well, not quite exactly," and Bill went off into a low, long, choking chuckle. "No, Hi," he went on, recovering himself with the same abruptness he used with his bronco, and looking at his friend with a solemn face, "your hayer ain't red, Hi; don't let any of your relatives persuade you to that. Tain't red! It may be blue, cerulean blue, or even purple, but red—!" He paused, but Hi, paying no attention to Bill's oration, took up the subject with enthusiasm.

"She kin ride—she's a regular buster to ride, ain't she, Bill?" Bill nodded. "She kin bunch cattle an' cut out an' yank a steer up to any cowboy on the range."

"Why, how big is she?"

"Big? Why she's just a kid! Tain't the bigness of her, it's the nerve. She's got the coldest kind of nerve you ever seen. Hain't she, Bill?" And again Bill nodded.

"'Member the day she dropped that steer, Bill?" Hi went on.

"What was that?" I asked, eager for a yarn.

"Oh, nuthin'," said Bill.

"Nuthin'!" retorted Hi. "Pretty big nuthin'!"

"What was it?" I urged.

"Oh, Bill here did some funny work at old Meredith's roundup, but he don't speak of it. He's shy, you see," and Hi grinned.

"Well, there ain't no occasion for your proceedin' onto that tact," said Bill disgustedly, and

Hi loyally refrained, so I have never yet got the rights of the story. But from what I did hear, I gathered that Bill, at the risk of his life, had pulled the Duke from under the hooves of a mad steer, and that little Gwen had, in the coolest possible manner, "sailed in on her bronco" and, by putting two bullets into the steer's head, had saved them both from great danger and perhaps from death, as the rest of the cattle were bearing down on them. Of course, Bill could never be persuaded to speak of the incident. A true Western man will never hesitate to tell you what he can do, but of what he has done he does not readily speak.

The only other item that Hi contributed to the sketch of Gwen was that her temper could blaze if the occasion demanded.

"'Member young Hill, Bill?"

Bill "'membered."

"Didn't she cut into him sudden? Served him right too."

"What did she do?"

"Cut him across the face with her riding crop in good style."

"What for?"

"Knockin' about her Indian Joe."

Joe was, as I came to learn, Ponka's son and Gwen's most devoted slave.

"Oh, she ain't no ice box."

"Yes," assented Bill. "She's a leetle swift."

Then, as if fearing he had been apologizing for her, added, with the air of one settling the question, "But she's good stock! She suits me!"

The Duke helped me see another side of her character.

"She's a remarkable child," he said, one day. "Wild and shy as a coyote, but fearless and with a heart full of passions. Meredith, the Old Timer, you know, has kept her up there among the hills. She sees no one but him and Ponka's Blackfeet relations, who treat her like a goddess and help to spoil her completely. She knows their lingo and their ways—goes off with them for a week at a time."

"What! With the Blackfeet?"

"Ponka and Joe, of course, go along, but even without them she is as safe as if surrounded by the Coldstream Guards."

"And at home?" I asked. "Has she any education? Can she read or write?"

"Not she. She can make her own dresses, moccasins, and leggings. She can cook and wash—

that is, when she feels in the mood. And she knows all about birds, animals, flowers, and that sort of thing, but—education! Why, she is hardly civilized!"

"What a shame!" I said. "How old is she?"

"Oh, a mere child—fourteen or fifteen, I imagine, but a woman in many things."

"And what does her father say to all this? Can he control her?"

"Control!" the Duke exclaimed. "Why, bless your soul, nothing in heaven or earth could control *her*. Wait till you see her stand with her proud little head thrown back, giving orders to Joe, and you will never again connect the idea of control with Gwen. She might be a princess for the pride of her. I've seen some too, in my day, but none to touch her for sheer, imperial pride, little Lucifer that she is."

"And how does her father stand her nonsense?" I asked, for I confess I was not much taken with the picture the Duke had drawn.

"Her father simply follows behind her and adores, as do all things that come near her, including her two dogs, Wolf and Loo, for either of which she would readily die if need be. Still," he added after a pause, "it *is* a shame, as you say.

She ought to know something of the civilization to which she belongs, and from which none of us can hope to escape." The Duke was silent for a few moments, and then added, with some hesitation: "Then, too, she is quite a pagan; never saw a prayer-book, you know."

And so it came about, mainly through the Duke's influence that I was engaged by the Old Timer to go up to his ranch every week and teach his daughter some basics of a lady's education.

My introduction was foretelling of the many things I was to suffer by way of that young woman before I had finished my lessons with her. The Old Timer had given careful directions as to the trail that would lead me to the canyon where he was to meet me. Up the Swan went the trail, winding ever downward into deeper and narrower canyons and up to open sunlit slopes, till suddenly it settled into a valley that began with great width and narrowed to a canyon whose rocky sides were filled out with shrubs and trailing vines and wet with trickling rivulets from the springs that oozed from the black, glistening rocks. This canyon was an eerie place of which ghostly tales were told from the old Blackfeet times. And to this day no Blackfoot will dare pass through this canyon after the moon has passed the western lip. But in the warm light of day, it was a good enough place, cool and sweet, and I lingered through, waiting for the Old Timer, who failed to appear.

The shadows began to darken the canyon's western sides. Out of the mouth of the canyon the trail climbed to a wide stretch of prairie that swept over soft hills on the left and down to the gleaming waters of Devil's Lake on the right. In the sunlight the lake lay like a gem radiant with many colors, black on the far side in the shadow of the pines, then deep blue and purple in the middle, and nearer, many shades of emerald that ran to the white, sandy beach. Right in front stood the ranch buildings, up on a slight rise and surrounded by a palisade of sturdy, pointed poles. This was the castle of the princess.

I rode to the open gate, then stopped and turned to look down at the colorful lake. Suddenly there was an awful roar, and my pony shot round upon his hind legs and deposited me on the ground and fled down the trail, pursued by two huge dogs that brushed past me as I fell. I was aroused from my amazement by a peal of laughter, shrill but full of music. Turning, I saw my pupil, as I guessed, standing at the head of a most beautiful pinto pony with a heavy cattle whip in her hand. I scrambled to my feet and said, "What are you laughing at? Why don't you call back your dogs? They will chase my pony beyond all reach."

She lifted her little head, shook back her masses of brown-red hair, looked at me as if I were quite beneath contempt and said, "No, they will kill him."

"Then," I said, for I was very angry, "I will kill them," pulling at the revolver in my belt.

"Then," she said, and for the first time I noticed her eyes, blue-black with gray rims, "I will kill you," and she whipped out an ugly-looking revolver. From her face I had no doubt that she would not hesitate to do as she had said. I changed my tactics, for I was worried about my pony, and with my best smile I said, "Can't you call them back? Won't they obey you?"

Her face changed in a moment.

"Is it your pony? Do you love him very much?"

"Dearly!" I lied, persuading myself of a sudden affection for the cranky little brute.

She sprang upon her pinto and set off down the trail. The pony was now coursing up and down the slopes, doubling like a rabbit, instinctively avoiding the canyon where he would be cornered. He was crazed with terror at the huge brutes that were silently but with awful and sure swiftness running him down.

The girl on the pinto whistled shrilly and called to her dogs: "Down, Wolf! Back, Loo!" But, running low, with long, stretched bodies, they didn't obey; they just sped on, gaining on the pony that now circled back toward the pinto. As they drew near in their circling, the girl urged her pinto to meet them, loosening her lariat as she went. As the pony neared the pinto he slackened his speed; immediately the nearer dog gathered herself in two short jumps and sprang for the pony's throat. But, even as she sprang, the lariat whirled round the girl's head and fell swift and sure about the dog's neck, and the next moment the dog lay choking upon the prairie. Her mate paused, looked back, and gave up the chase. But dire vengeance overtook them, for, like one possessed, the girl fell upon them with her whip and beat them one after the other till, in pity for the brutes, I intervened.

"They will do as I say or I will kill them! I will kill them!" she cried, raging and stamping.

"Better shoot them," I suggested, pulling out my pistol.

Immediately she flung herself upon the one that moaned and whined at her feet, crying, "If you dare! If you dare!" Then she burst into passionate sobbing. "You bad Loo! You bad, dear old Loo! But you *were* bad . . . you *know* you were bad!" and so she went on with her arms about Loo's neck till Loo, whining and quivering with love and delight, and Wolf, standing majestically near, broke into short howls of impatience for his turn of caressing. They made a strange group, those three wild things, equally fierce and passionate in hate and in love.

Suddenly the girl remembered me, and standing up she said, half ashamed, "They always obey *me*. They are *mine*, but they kill any strange thing that comes in through the gate. They are allowed to."

"It is a pleasant whim."

"What?"

"I mean, isn't that dangerous to strangers?"

"Oh, no one ever comes alone, except the Duke. And they keep off the wolves."

"The Duke comes, does he?"

"Yes!" and her eyes lit up. "He is my friend. He calls me his 'princess,' and he teaches me things and tells me stories, wonderful stories!"

I looked in wonder at her face, so gentle, so girlish, and tried to think back to the picture of the girl who a few moments before had so coolly threatened to shoot me and had so furiously beaten her dogs.

I kept her talking about the Duke as we walked back to the gate, watching her face. It was not beautiful; it was too thin, and the mouth was too large. But the teeth were good, and the blue-black eyes looked straight at you—true eyes, and brave, whether in love or in war. Her hair was her glory. Red it was, in spite of Hi's denial, but of such a marvelous, indescribable shade that in certain lights, as she rode over the prairie, it streamed behind her like a purple banner. A most confusing and bewildering color, but quite in keeping with the nature of the owner.

She gave her pinto to Joe and, standing at the door, welcomed me with a dignity and graciousness that made me think that the Duke was not far wrong when he named her "Princess."

The door opened upon the main or living room. It was a long apartment, with low ceiling and walls of hewn logs chinked and plastered and all beautifully whitewashed and clean. The tables, chairs, and benches were all homemade. On the floor were magnificent skins of wolf, bear, musk ox, and mountain goat. The walls were decorated with heads and horns of deer and mountain sheep, eagles' wings, and a beautiful breast of a loon, which Gwen had shot and of which she was very proud. At one end of the room a huge stone fireplace stood radiant in its summer decorations of ferns, grasses, and wildflowers. At the other end a door opened into another room, smaller and richly furnished with relics of former grandeur.

Everything was clean and well kept. Every nook, shelf, and corner was decked with flowers and ferns from the canyon.

A strange house it was, full of curious contrasts, but it fit this quaint child who now welcomed me with such gracious courtesy that the incident of my arrival was completely forgotten.

10

Gwen's First Prayers

It was with hesitation, almost with fear, that I began with Gwen. But even had I been able to foresee the endless series of frustrations through which she put me, I still would have accepted the challenge. For the child, with all her willfulness, her temper tantrums, and her pride, made me, along with everyone else who met her, her willing slave.

Her lessons went on, brilliantly, or not at all, according to her whim. She learned to read with extraordinary speed, for she was eager to know more of the thrilling tales of the world which the Duke had told her. Writing she abhorred. She had no one to write to. Why should she cramp her fingers over these crooked little marks? But she mastered with hardly a struggle the mysteries of mathematics, for she would have to sell her cattle, and "dad doesn't know when they are cheating."

Gwen's ideas of education were purely utilitarian, and what did not appear immediately useful she refused to mess with. And so all through the following long winter she stretched my patience with her iron-willed ways. My appeals to her father were useless. She would wind her long, thin arms about his neck and let her waving red hair float over him until the old man was quite helpless to exert any authority. The Duke could do the most with her. To please him she would struggle with her crooked letters for an hour at a time, but even his influence and authority had its limits.

"Must I?" she said one day, in answer to a demand of his for more faithful study. And throwing up her proud little head, and shaking back her streaming red hair, she looked straight at him from her blue-gray eyes and asked "Why?"

The Duke looked back at her with his slight smile for a few moments and then said in cold, even tones, "I really don't know why," and turned his back on her.

Immediately she sprang at him, shook him by the arm, and, quivering with anger, cried, "You are not to speak to me like that, and you are not to turn your back that way!"

"What a little princess she is," he said admiringly, "and what a time she will give herself some day!" The he added, smiling sadly, "Was I rude, Gwen? Then I am sorry."

Her rage was gone. Too proud to show her feelings, she just looked at him with softening eyes and then sat down to the work she had refused.

This was after the arrival of the Pilot at Swan Creek, and, as the Duke rode home with me that night, after a long silence he said with hesitation, "She ought to have some religion, poor child; she will grow up a perfect little devil. The Pilot might be of service if you could bring him up. Women need that sort of thing; it refines them, you know."

"Would she have him?" I asked.

"Good question," he replied, doubtfully. "You might suggest it to her."

Which I did, introducing somewhat clumsily the Duke's name.

"The Duke says he is to make me good!" she cried. "I won't have him, I hate him and you too!" And for that day she refused all lessons, and when the Duke next appeared she greeted him with, "I won't have your old Pilot, and I don't want to be good, and . . . and . . . you think he's no good yourself," at which the Duke winced, slightly.

"How do you know? I never said so!"

"You laughed at him to dad one day."

"Did I?" said the Duke. "Then I hasten to assure you that I have changed my mind. He is a good, brave man."

"He falls off his horse," she said with contempt.

"I rather think he sticks on now," replied the Duke, repressing a smile.

"Besides," she went on, "he's just a kid; Bill said so."

"Well, he could be older," acknowledged the Duke, "but in that he is steadily improving."

"Anyway," she said with an air of finality, "he is not to come here."

But the Pilot did come, and under her own escort, one storm-filled August evening.

"I found him in the creek," she defiantly announced, marching in the half-drowned Pilot.

"I think I could have crossed," he said apologetically, "for Louis was getting on his feet again."

"No, you wouldn't," she protested. "You would have been down in the canyon by now, and you ought to be thankful."

"So I am," he quickly agreed, "very! But," he added, unwilling to give up his contention, "I have crossed the Swan before."

"Not when it was in flood."

"Yes, when it was in flood, higher than now."

"Not where the banks are rocky."

"No-o!" he hesitated.

"There, then, you *would* have been drowned but for my lariat!" she cried triumphantly. To this he doubtfully assented.

They were much alike, high in temper, in enthusiasm, in vivid imagination, and in sensitive feelings. When the Old Timer came in, Gwen triumphantly introduced the Pilot as having been rescued from a watery grave by her lariat, and again they fought out the possibilities of drowning and of escape until Gwen finally was appeased by the extreme expressions of gratitude on the part of the Pilot. The Old Timer was perplexed. He was afraid to offend Gwen and yet unwilling to be cordial to her guest. The Pilot was quick to feel this, and, soon after supper, rose to go. Gwen's disappointment showed in her face.

"Ask him to stay, Dad," she whispered. But the half-hearted invitation acted like a spur, and the Pilot was determined to set off.

"There's a bad storm coming," she said, "and besides," she added, with authority, "you can't cross the Swan."

"I can't cross the Swan, eh?" And with that, even the most earnest prayers of the Old Timer could not have held him back.

We all went down to see him cross, Gwen leading her pinto. The Swan was far over its banks, and in the middle, a torrent running swift and strong. Louis snorted, refused, and finally plunged. Bravely he swam, till the swift-running water struck him, and over he went on his side, throwing his rider into the water. The Pilot kept his head, and, holding by the stirrups, paddled along by Louis's side. When they were halfway across, Louis saw that he had no chance of making the landing, so, like a sensible horse, he turned and made for the shore. Here, too, the banks were high, and the pony began to grow discouraged.

"Let him float down farther!" shrieked Gwen, in anxious excitement. Urging her pinto down the bank, she coaxed the struggling pony down the stream to a spot opposite a shelf of rock level with the high water. Then she threw her lariat, and, catching Louis about the neck and the horn of his saddle, she held taut, till, half drowned, he scrambled up the bank, dragging the Pilot with him.

"Oh, I'm so glad!" she said, almost tearfully. "You see, you couldn't get across."

The Pilot staggered to his feet, took a step toward her, gasped out, "I can!" and pitched headlong onto the ground. With a little cry she ran to him, and turned him over on his back. In a few moments he revived, sat up, and looked about stupidly.

"Where's Louis?" he asked, with his face toward the swollen stream.

"Safe enough," she answered; "but you must come in, the rain is just going to pour."

But the Pilot seemed possessed.

"No, I'm going across," he said, rising.

Gwen was greatly distressed.

"But your poor horse," she said, cleverly changing her tack, "he's tired out."

The Old Timer now joined in, urging him to stay till the storm was past. So, with a final look at the stream, the Pilot turned toward the house.

Of course I knew what would happen. Before the evening was over he had captured the household. The moment he appeared with dry things on he went straight to the organ that had stood for ten years closed and silent, opened it, and began to play.

As the Pilot played and sang song after song, the Old Timer's eyes began to glisten under his shaggy brows. But when he dropped into the exquisite Irish melody, "Oft in the Stilly Night," the old man drew a hard breath and groaned out, "It was her mother's song," and from that time the Pilot had him completely won over.

The Pilot eased into the old hymn "Nearer, My God, to Thee," after which he simply said,

"May we have prayers?" He looked at Gwen, but she gazed blankly at him and then at her father.

"What does he mean, Dad?"

It was pitiful to see the old man's face grow slowly red under the deep tan as he said, "You may, sir. There's been none here for many years, and the worse for us." The old man rose slowly, went into the inner room, and returned with a Bible.

"It's her mother's," he said, in a voice deep with emotion. "I put it in her trunk the day I laid her out yonder under the pines."

The Pilot, without looking at him, rose and reverently took the book in both his hands and gently said, "It was a sad day for you, but for her . . ." He paused. "You did not hate her for leaving you?"

"Not now, but then, yes. I wanted her, we needed her." The Old Timer's tears were flowing.

The Pilot put his hand caressingly upon the old man's shoulder as if he had been his father and said in his clear, sweet voice, "Some day you will go to her."

On this scene poor Gwen gazed with eyes wide open with amazement and a kind of fear. She had never seen her father weep since the awful day that she could never forget, when he had knelt in dumb agony beside the bed on which her mother lay white and still. Her father had not even noticed her until, climbing up, she tried to make her mother waken and hear her cries. Then he had caught her up in his arms, pressing her with tears and great sobs to his heart. Tonight she seemed to feel that something was wrong. She went and stood by her father, and stroking his gray hair, she said:

"What is he saying, Daddy? Is he making you cry?" She looked at the Pilot defiantly.

"No, no, child," said the old man, hastily, "sit here and listen."

And while the storm raged outside, we three sat listening to that ancient story of love unspeakable. And, as the words fell like sweet music on our ears, the old man sat with eyes that looked far away, while the child listened with devouring eagerness.

"Is it a fairy tale, Daddy?" she asked when the Pilot paused. "It isn't true, is it?" and her voice had a pleading note hard for the old man to bear.

"Yes, yes, my child," he said, brokenly. "God forgive me!"

"Of course it's true," said the Pilot, quietly. "I'll read it all to you tomorrow. It's a beautiful story!"

"No," she said imperiously, "tonight. Read it now! Go on!" she said, stamping her foot. "Don't you hear me?"

The Pilot gazed in surprise at her, and then turning to the old man, he said, "Shall I?"

The Old Timer simply nodded and the reading went on. Those were not my best days, and the faith of my childhood was not as it had been, but, as the Pilot carried us through those matchless scenes of selfless love and service, the rapt wonder in the child's face as she listened and the appeal in her voice as she cried to us, "Is *that* true too? Is it *all* true?" made it impossible for me to hesitate in my answer. And I was glad to find it easy to give my firm adherence to the truth of all that wondrous tale. And, as it dawned upon the Pilot that the story he was reading, so old to him and to all he had ever met, was new to one in that listening group, his face began to glow and his eyes to blaze, and he saw and showed me things that night I had never seen before, nor have I seen them since. The great figure of the Gospels lived and moved before our eyes. We saw Him speak His marvelous teaching, we felt the throbbing excitement of the crowds that pressed against Him.

Suddenly the Pilot stopped, turned over the pages, and began again: "And He led them out as far as Bethany. And He lifted up His hands and blessed them. And it came to pass as He blessed them He was parted from them and a cloud received Him out of their sight."

There was silence for some minutes, then Gwen said, "Where did He go?"

"Up into heaven," answered the Pilot, simply.

"That's where Mother is," she said to her father, who nodded in reply.

"Does He know?" she asked. The old man looked distressed.

"Of course He does," said the Pilot, "and she sees Him all the time."

"Oh, Daddy!" she cried, "isn't that good?"

But the old man only hid his face in his hands and groaned.

"Yes," went on the Pilot, "and He sees us, too, and hears us speak, and knows our thoughts."

Again the look of wonder and fear came into her eyes, but she didn't say a word. The experiences of the evening had made the world new to her. It could never be the same to her again. It gave me an odd feeling to see her stand helplessly looking on as we three kneeled to pray. Finally, not knowing what to do, she sank beside her father, and winding her arms about his neck, clung to him as the words of prayer were spoken into the ear of Him whom no man can see.

Those were Gwen's first "prayers," and in them Gwen's part was small, for fear and wonder filled her heart. But the day was to come, and all too soon, when she would have to pour out her soul in a tearful downpour.

11

Gwen's Challenge

Gwen was undoubtedly wild and, as the Sky Pilot said, willful and wicked. Even Bronco Bill and Hi Kendal would say so, without lessening one jot of their admiration for her. For fourteen years she had lived chiefly with wild things. Cattle, deer, coyotes, jackrabbits, and timber wolves were her friends and instructors. From these she learned her wild ways. She loved her home, the rolling prairie and all things that moved upon it. All summer long she spent her days riding up and over the range alone, or with her father, or Joe, or, best of all, with the Duke, her hero and her friend. So she grew up strong, wholesome, and self-reliant, fearing nothing alive and as untamed as a yearling range colt.

It was a great day for her when she fished the Sky Pilot out of the Swan and brought him home, and the night of Gwen's first "prayers," when she heard for the first time the story of the Man of Nazareth, was the best of all her nights up to that time. All through the winter, the Pilot went over and over that story with her and the old man, till a whole new world of mystery lay open to her imagination and became the home of new and great realities. She was rich in imagination, and when the Pilot read John Bunyan's *Pilgrim's Progress,* an old book of her mother's, she moved and lived beside the hero of that tale.

The Pilot himself was a new and wholesome experience for her. He was the first thing she had yet encountered that refused to submit and the first human being that had failed to fall down and "worship" her. There was something in him that would not *always* yield to her personality, and he met her temper and pride with surprise and sometimes with a pity that veered toward contempt. She was not pleased with this and as

GWEN'S CHALLENGE 111

a result frequently let him feel the full force of her wrath.

One of Gwen's outbursts is stamped upon my mind, not only because of its unusual violence, but chiefly because of the events that followed. The original cause of her rage was some insignificant misdeed of Joe, but when I came upon the scene it was the Pilot who occupied her attention. The slightly sorrowful expression on his face seemed to stir her up.

"How dare you look at me like that!" she cried.

"How very extraordinary that you can't keep hold of yourself better," he answered.

"I can!" she stamped, "and I will do as I like!"

"It is a great pity," he said, with provoking calm, "and besides, it is weak and silly." His words were unfortunate.

"Weak!" she gasped, when her breath came back to her. "Weak!"

"Yes," he said, "very weak and childish."

Then she could have cheerfully put him to a slow and cruel death. When she had recovered a little, she cried vehemently, "I'm not weak! I'm strong! I'm stronger than you are! I'm strong as . . . as . . . a man!"

I didn't think she meant any insinuation, but the Pilot ignored it and went on. "You're not strong enough to keep your temper down." And as she had no ready reply, he went on, "And really, Gwen, it is not right. You must not go on in this way."

Again his words were unfortunate.

"*Must* not!" she screamed, adding an inch to her height. "Who says so?"

"God!" was the simple, short answer.

She was greatly taken back, and she gave a quick glance over her shoulder as if to see Him who would dare to say *must not* to her. Recovering, she answered sullenly, "I don't care!"

"Don't care for God?" The Pilot's voice was quiet and solemn, but something in his manner angered her, and she blazed forth again.

"I don't care for anyone, and I *will* do as I like."

The Pilot looked at her sadly for a moment and then said slowly, "Some day, Gwen, you will not be able to do as you like."

I remember well the settled defiance in her tone and manner as she took a step nearer him and answered in a voice trembling with passion, "Listen! I have always done as I like, and I shall do as I like till I die!" And she rushed out of the house and down toward the canyon, her refuge from all disturbing things, and chiefly from herself.

I could not shake off the impression her words made on me. "Pretty direct, that," I said to the Pilot, as we rode away. "The declaration may be philosophically correct, but it rings uncommonly like a challenge to the Almighty. Throws down the gauntlet, so to speak."

Within a week her challenge was accepted, and how fiercely and gallantly did she struggle to make it good!

The Duke brought me the news, and as he told me the story his cheerful, careless self-command for once was gone. For in the gloom of the canyon where he overtook me I could see his face gleaming out ghastly white, and even his iron nerve could not keep the tremor from his voice.

"I've just sent up the doctor," was his answer to my greeting. "I looked for you last night, couldn't find you, and so I rode off to the fort."

"What's up?" I said with fear in my heart, for no light thing moved the Duke.

"Haven't you heard? It's Gwen," he said, and the next minute or two he gave to Jingo, who was indulging in a series of unexpected plunges. When Jingo was brought down, the Duke was master of himself and gave me his report with a conscious attempt at self-control.

Gwen, on her father's buckskin bronco, had gone with the Duke to the big plain above the cut-bank ravine where Joe was herding the cattle. The day was hot and a storm was in the air. They found Joe riding up and down, singing to keep the cattle quiet, but having a hard time holding the bunch from breaking. While the Duke was riding around the far side of the bunch, a cry from Gwen arrested his attention. Joe was in trouble. His horse, a half-broke cayuse, had stumbled into a badger hole and had bolted, leaving Joe to the mercy of the cattle. Joe kept his head and walked slowly out, till all at once a young cow began to bawl and to paw the ground. In another minute one and then another of the cattle began to toss their heads and bunch and bellow till the whole herd of two hundred were after Joe. Then Joe lost his head and ran. Immediately the whole herd broke into a thundering gallop with heads and tails aloft and horns rattling like the loading of a regiment of rifles.

"In spite of my most frantic warnings and signalings, right into the face of that mad, thundering mass rode that little girl," the Duke said. "Nerve! I have some myself, but I couldn't have done it. She swung her horse round Joe and sailed out with him, with the heard bellowing at the tail of her bronco. I've seen some daring things in my day, but for sheer cool bravery nothing touches that."

"How did it end? Did they run them down?" I asked, horrified of such a result.

"No, they crowded her toward the ravine, and she was edging them off and was almost past, when they came to a place where the edge veered inward, and her iron-mouthed brute wouldn't swerve, but went pounding on, broke through the bank, and plunged. She couldn't spring free because of Joe, and she pitched headlong over the edge, while the cattle went thundering past. I flung myself off Jingo and slid down somehow into the sand, thirty feet below. Here was Joe safe enough, but the bronco lay with a broken leg, and half under him was Gwen. She hardly knew she was hurt, but waved her hand to me and cried out, 'Wasn't that a race? I couldn't swing this hardheaded beast. Get me out.' But even as she spoke the light faded from her eyes, she stretched out her hands to me, saying faintly, 'Oh Duke,' and lay back white and still. We put a bullet into the buckskin's head and carried Gwen home in our jackets, and there she lies without a sound."

The Duke was deeply affected. I had never seen him show any sign of grief before, but as he finished the story he stood shaking. He read the surprise in my face and said, "Look here, old chap, don't think me quite a fool. You can't know what that little girl has done for me these years. Her trust in me—it is extraordinary how utterly she trusts me—somehow held me up to my best. She is the one bright spot in my life in this blessed country. Everyone else thinks me a pleasant or unpleasant kind of fiend."

I protested rather faintly.

"Oh, don't worry your conscience," he answered, with a slight return of his old smile. "A fuller knowledge would only justify the opinion." Then, after a pause, he added: "But if Gwen goes, I must pull out; I could not stand it."

As we rode up, the doctor came out.

"Well, what do you think?" the Duke asked.

"Can't say yet," replied the old doctor, gruff with long army practice, "bad enough. Good night."

But the Duke's hand fell upon his shoulder with a grip that must have got to the bone, and in a husky voice he asked, "Will she live?"

The doctor squirmed but could not shake off that crushing grip.

"Here, you young tiger, let go! What do you think I am made of?" he cried angrily. "I didn't suppose I was coming to a bear's den, or I should have brought a gun."

It was only by the most complete apology that the Duke could mollify the doctor sufficiently to get his opinion.

"No, she will not die! Great bit of stuff! Better she should die, perhaps! But can't say yet for two weeks. Now remember," he added sharply, looking into the Duke's woe-stricken face, "her spirits must be kept up. I have lied most fully and cheerfully to them inside; you must do the same," and the doctor strode away, calling out, "Joe! Here, Joe! Where is he gone? Joe, I say! Extraordinary selection Providence makes at times; we could have spared that lazy half-breed with pleasure! Joe! Oh, here you are! Where in thunder . . . ?" But here the doctor stopped abruptly. The agony in the dark face before him was too much even for the gruff doctor. Straight and stiff,

Joe stood by the horse's head till the doctor had mounted, then with a great effort he said:

"Little miss, she go dead?"

"Dead!" called out the doctor, glancing at the open window. "Why, bless your old copper carcass, no! Gwen will show you yet how to rope a steer."

Joe took a step nearer and lowering his tone said, "You speak me truth? Me man, me no papoose." The piercing black eyes searched the doctor's face. The doctor hesitated a moment, and then, with an air of great candor, said cheerily, "That's all right, Joe. Miss Gwen will cut circles round your old cayuse yet. But remember," and the doctor was very impressive, "you must make her laugh every day."

Joe folded his arms across his breast and stood like a statue till the doctor rode away, then turning to us he said, "Him good man, eh?"

"Good man," answered the Duke, adding, "but remember, Joe, what he told you to do. Must make her laugh every day."

Poor Joe! Humor was not his forte, and his attempts in this direction in the weeks that followed would have been humorous were they not so pathetic. How I did my part I cannot tell.

Those weeks are to me now like the memory of an ugly nightmare. The ghostly old man moving out and in of his little daughter's room in useless, dumb agony; Ponka's woe-stricken Indian face; Joe's unusual but loyal attempts at fun-making, and the Duke's unvarying and invincible cheeriness; these furnish light and shade for the picture my memory brings me of Gwen in those days.

For the first two weeks she was simply heroic. She bore her pain without a groan and submitted to the imprisonment that to her was harder than the pain. Joe, the Duke, and I carried out our instructions with careful exactness. She never doubted, and we never let her doubt but that in a few weeks she would be on the pinto's back again and after the cattle. She made us give our word for this till it seemed as if she must have read the falsehoods in our eyes.

"To lie cheerfully with her eyes upon one's face calls for more than I possess," said the Duke one day. "The doctor should supply us tonics. It is an arduous task."

She believed us absolutely; she made plans for the fall roundup and for hunts and rides till one's heart grew sick. As to the ethical problem involved, I decline to express an opinion, but we had no need to wait for our punishment. Her trust in us, her eager and confident expectation of the return of her happy, free outdoor life, these brought to us their own adequate punishment for every false assurance we gave. And how bright and brave she was those first days! How resolute to get back to the world of air and light outside!

But she had need of all her brightness and courage and resolution before she was done with her long fight.

12

Gwen's Canyon

Gwen's hope and bright courage, in spite of all her pain, were wonderful to witness. But from the day of the doctors' consultation, all this cheery hope, courage, and patience were snuffed out, leaving darkness to settle down in that sickroom.

The verdict was clear and final. The old doctor, who loved Gwen as his own, was inclined to hope against hope. But Fawcett, the clever young doctor from the distant town, was positive in his opinion. The scene is clear to me now, after many years. We three stood in the outer room; the Duke and her father were with Gwen. So earnest was the discussion that none of us heard the door open just as young Fawcett was saying in incisive tones, "No! I can see no hope! The child can never walk again."

There was a cry behind us.

"What! Never walk again! It's a lie!" There stood the Old Timer, white, fierce, shaking.

"Hush!" said the old doctor, pointing at the open door. He was too late. Even as he spoke, there came from the inner room a wild, unearthly cry as some dying thing, and, as we stood gazing at one another with awe-stricken faces, we heard Gwen's voice as in quick, sharp pain.

"Daddy! Daddy! Come! What do they say? Tell me, Daddy. It isn't true! It isn't true! Look at me, Daddy!"

She pulled up her father's haggard face from the bed.

"Oh, Daddy, Daddy, you know it's true. Never walk again!"

She turned with a pitiful cry to the Duke, who stood white and stiff with arms drawn tight across his chest on the other side of the bed.

"Oh, Duke, did you hear them? You told me to be brave, and I tried not to cry when they hurt me. But I can't be brave! Can I, Duke? Oh, Duke! Never to ride again!"

She stretched out her hands to him. But the Duke, leaning over her and holding her hands fast in his, could only say over and over: "Don't, Gwen! Don't, Gwen dear!"

"Oh, Duke! Must I always lie here? Must I? Why must I?"

"God knows," answered the Duke bitterly, under his breath.

She caught at the word.

"Does He?" she cried, eagerly. Then she paused suddenly, turned to me, and said, "Do you remember he said some day I could not do as I liked?"

I was puzzled.

"The Pilot," she snapped. "Don't you remember? And I said I should do as I liked till I died."

I nodded my head and said, "But you know you didn't mean it."

"But I did, and I do," she stated, with passionate vehemence, "and I will do as I like! I will not lie here! I will ride! I will! I will! I will!" and she struggled up, clenched her fists, and sank back faint and weak. It was not a pleasant sight. Her rage against that Unseen Omnipotence was so defiant and so helpless.

Those were dreadful weeks to Gwen and to all about her. The constant pain could not break her proud spirit; she shed no tears, but she fretted and chafed and grew more imperiously exacting every day. She drove Ponka and Joe like slaves, and even her father she impatiently banished from her room when he could not understand her wishes. Only the Duke could please or bring her any cheer, and he eventually began to feel that the day was not far off when he too would fail, and the thought filled him with despair. Her pain was hard to bear, but harder than the pain was her longing for the open air and the open, breeze-swept prairie. But most pitiful of all were the days when in sheer, uncontrollable unrest, she would beg to be taken down into the canyon.

"Oh, it is so cool and shady," she would plead, "and the flowers up in the rocks and the vines and things are all so lovely. I am always better there. I know I should be better," till a distraught Duke would come to me and wonder aloud what the end would be.

One day, when the strain had been more terrible than usual, the Duke rode down to me and said:

"Look here, this thing can't go on. Where has the Pilot gone? Why doesn't he stay where he belongs? I wish to heaven he would get through with his absurd rambling."

"He's gone where he was sent," I replied shortly. "You don't set much store by him when he does come around. He is gone on an exploring trip through the Dog Lake country. He'll be back by the end of next week."

"I say, bring him up for heaven's sake; he may be of some use, and anyway it will be a new face for the poor child." Then he added, rather penitently: "I fear this thing is getting on my nerves. She almost drove me out today. Don't hold it against me, old chap."

It was a new thing to hear the Duke confess his need of any man, much less admit a fault. I felt my eyes begin to water, but I snapped, "You be hanged! I'll bring the Pilot up when he comes."

It was wonderful how we had all come to confide in the Pilot during his year of missionary work among us. Somehow the cowboy's name of "Sky Pilot" seemed to express better than anything else the place he held with us. When, in their dark hours, any of the fellows felt in need of help to strike the "upward trail," they went to the Pilot. And so the name first given in fun came to be the name that expressed most truly the deep feeling these rough, big-hearted men had for him.

When the Pilot came home I carefully prepared him for his trial, telling all that Gwen had suffered and striving to make him feel how desperate was her case when even the Duke had to confess himself beaten. He did not seem sufficiently impressed. Then I pictured for him all her fierce willfulness and fretful moods, her impatience with those who loved her and were wearing themselves out for her. I concluded, "she doesn't care a rush for anything in heaven or earth and will yield neither to man nor God."

The Pilot's eyes had grown intense as I talked, but he only answered quietly, "What could you expect?"

"Well, I do think she might show some signs of gratitude and some kindness toward those ready to die for her."

"Oh, you do!" said he, with high scorn. "You all combine to ruin her temper and disposition with flattery and giving in to her every whim, right or wrong. You smile at her pride and encourage her strong determination, and then not only wonder at the results, but blame her, poor child, for all. Oh, you are a fine lot, the Duke and all of you!"

He had a most exasperating ability for putting one in the wrong, and I could only think of an appropriate response long after the opportunity for making it had passed. I wondered what the Duke would say to this. All the following day, which was Sunday, I could see that Gwen was on the Pilot's mind. He was struggling with the problem of pain.

Monday morning found us on the way to the Old Timer's ranch. And what a morning it was; how beautiful our world seemed! About us rolled the velvet hills, behind us the broad prairie, and before, the great mountains that lay across the horizon and thrust their white, sunlit peaks into the sky. On the hillsides and down in the sheltering hollows we could see the bunches of cattle and horses feeding on the rich grasses. High above, the sky was cloudless and blue, and the sun poured floods of radiant yellow light.

As we followed the trail that wound up and

into the heart of these hills and ever nearer to the purple mountains, the morning breeze swept down to meet us, bearing a thousand scents, and filling us with its own fresh life.

Through all this mingling beauty we rode with hardly a word, every minute adding to our delight, but also with thoughts of the little room, where shut in from all this outside glory, lay Gwen. This must have been in the Pilot's mind, for he suddenly held up his horse and burst out: "Poor Gwen, how she loves all this!—it is her very life. How can she help fretting the heart out of her? To see this no more!" He flung himself off his bronco and said, as if thinking aloud, "It is too awful! Oh, it is cruel! I don't wonder at her! God help me, what can I say to her?"

He threw himself down on the grass and turned over on his face. After a few minutes he appealed to me, and his face was troubled.

"How can one go to her? It seems to me sheerest mockery to speak of patience and submission to a wild young thing from whom all this is suddenly snatched forever—and this was very life to her."

Then he sprang up and we rode hard for an hour, till we came to the mouth of the canyon.

Here the trail grew difficult and we came to a walk. As we went down into the cool depths the spirit of the canyon came to meet us and took the Pilot in its grip. He rode in front, feasting his eyes on all the wonders in that storehouse of beauty. Trees of many kinds deepened the shadows of the canyon. And throughout, the Little Swan sang its song to rocks and flowers and the overhanging trees, a song of many tones, deep-booming where it took its first sheer plunge, chattering where it threw itself down the ragged rocks, and murmuring where it lingered about the roots of the elms. A cool, sweet, soothing place it was, with all its shades and sounds and with sharp, quick sunbeams dancing down through the trees and splashing the secret places in light. No wonder the Pilot, drawing a deep breath as he touched the prairie sod again, said:

"That does me good. It is better at times even than the sunny hills. This was Gwen's best spot."

I saw that the canyon had done its work with him. His face was strong and calm as the hills on a summer morning, and with this face he looked in upon Gwen. It was one of her bad days and one of her bad moods, but like a warm and gentle breeze he entered the little room.

"Oh, Gwen!" he cried, without a word of greeting, much less of commiseration, "we have had such a ride!" And he spread out the sunlit hills before her, till I could feel their very breezes in my face. This the Duke had never dared to do, fearing to grieve her with pictures of a place that she could never again see. But as the Pilot talked, Gwen was out again on her beloved hills, breathing their fresh, sunny air, filling her heart with their delights, till her eyes grew bright and the lines of fretting smoothed out of her face and she forgot her pain. Then, before she could remember, he had her down in the canyon, feasting her heart with its airs, sights, and sounds. The black, glistening rocks, covered with moss and trailing vines, the great elms and low cedars, the clematis and columbine hanging from the rocky nooks, and the violets and maidenhair deeply bedded in their mosses. All this and far more he showed her with a touch so light as not to shake the morning dew from leaf or frond, and with a voice so soft and full of music until it filled our hearts with the canyon's mingling sounds.

As I looked upon her face, I said to myself,

"Dear old Pilot! for this I will always love you well." As poor Gwen listened, the rapture of it drew big tears down her cheeks—no longer sun-browned, but white, and for that day at least the dull, dead weariness was lifted from her heart.

13

The Canyon Flowers

The Pilot's first visit to Gwen had been a triumph. But none knew better than he that the fight was still to come, for deep in Gwen's heart were thoughts whose pain made her forget all other.

"Did God let me fall?" she asked abruptly one day.

The Pilot knew the fight was on, but looking fearlessly into her eyes he answered, "Yes, Gwen dear."

"Why did He let me fall?" she said deliberately.

"I don't know, Gwen," said the Pilot steadily. "He knows."

"And does He know I will never ride again? Does He know how long the days are, and the nights when I can't sleep? Does He know?"

"Yes, Gwen dear," said the Pilot, and tears were standing in his eyes, though his voice never wavered.

"Are you sure He knows?" The voice was painfully intense.

"Listen to me, Gwen . . ." began the Pilot, in great distress, but she cut him short.

"Are you quite sure He knows? Answer me!" she cried with her old dominance.

"Yes, Gwen, He knows all about you."

"Then what do you think of Him, just because He's big and strong, treating a little girl that way?" Then she added, viciously, "I hate Him! I don't care! I hate Him!"

The Pilot did not wince. I wondered how he would solve that problem, puzzling not only Gwen, but her father and the Duke, and all of us—the *why* of human pain.

"Gwen," said the Pilot, as if changing the subject, "did it hurt to put on the plaster jacket?"

"You bet!" said Gwen, lapsing in her English,

as the Duke was not present. "It was worse than anything—awful! They had to straighten me out, you know." She shuddered at the memory of that pain.

"What a pity your father or the Duke was not here!" said the Pilot, earnestly.

"Why, they were both here!"

"What a cruel shame!" burst out the Pilot. "Don't they care for you any more?"

"Of course they do," said Gwen, indignantly.

"Why didn't they stop the doctors from hurting you so cruelly?"

"Why, they let the doctors. It is going to help me to sit up and perhaps to walk about a little," answered Gwen, with blue-gray eyes open wide.

"Oh," said the Pilot, "it was very mean to stand by and see you hurt like that."

"Why, you silly," replied Gwen, "they want my back to get straight and strong."

"Oh, then they didn't do it just for fun, for nothing?" said the Pilot.

Gwen gazed at him in amazed and speechless wrath, and he went on: "I mean they love you though they let you be hurt, or rather they let the doctors hurt you *because* they loved you and wanted to make you better."

Gwen kept her eyes fixed with curious seriousness on his face till the light began to dawn. "Do you mean," she began slowly, "that though God let me fall, He loves me?"

The Pilot nodded; he could not trust his voice.

"I wonder if that can be true," she said, as if to herself.

Soon we said good-bye and left—the Pilot, limp and voiceless, but I triumphant, for I began to see a little light for Gwen.

But the fight was by no means over; indeed, it had hardly begun. For when the autumn came, with its misty, purple days, the most glorious of all days in the cattle country, the old restlessness came back and with it, fierce denial. Then came the day of the roundup. Why should she have to stay while all went after the cattle? The Duke would have remained, but she impatiently sent him away. She was weary and heartsick, and, worst of all, she began to feel her life a burden to others. I was much relieved when the Pilot came in fresh and bright, waving a bunch of wildflowers in his hand.

"I thought they were all gone," he exclaimed. "Where do you think I found them? Right down by the big elm root," and, though he saw by the gloom of her face that the storm was coming, he went bravely on picturing the canyon in all the splendor of its autumn dress.

But the Pilot's spell would not work. Her heart was out on the sloping hills, where the cattle were bunching with tossing heads and rattling horns, and it was in a voice very bitter that she cried, "Oh, I am sick of all this! I want to ride! I want to see the cattle and the men and . . . and . . . and all the things outside."

The Pilot was cowboy enough to know the longing that tugged at her heart for one wild race after the calves or steers, but he could only say, "Wait, Gwen. Try to be patient."

"I am patient; at least I have been patient for two whole months, and it's no use, and I don't believe God cares one bit!"

"Yes, He does, Gwen, more than any of us," replied the Pilot.

"No, He does not care," she answered, with angry emphasis, and the Pilot made no reply.

"Perhaps," she went on, hesitatingly, "He's angry because I said I didn't care for Him, you remember? That was very wicked. But don't you think I'm punished nearly enough now? You made me very angry, and I didn't really mean it."

Poor Gwen! God had grown to be very real to her during these weeks of pain, and very terrible. The Pilot looked down a moment into her eyes, grown so big and pitiful, and hurriedly dropping to his knees beside the bed he said, in a very unsteady voice, "Oh, Gwen, Gwen, He's not like that. Don't you remember how Jesus was with the poor sick people? That's what He's like."

"Could Jesus make me well?"

"Yes, Gwen."

"Then why doesn't He?" she asked. There was no impatience now, only trembling anxiety as she went on in a timid voice: "I asked Him to, over and over, and said I would wait two months, and now it's more than three. Are you quite sure He hears now?" She raised herself on her elbow and gazed searchingly into the Pilot's face. I was glad it was not into mine. As she uttered the words "Are you quite sure?" one felt that things were in the balance.

I could not help looking at the Pilot with intense anxiety. What would he answer? The Pilot gazed out the window for a few moments. How long the silence seemed! Then, turning, he looked into the eyes that searched his so steadily and answered simply, "Yes, Gwen, I am quite sure!"

Then, with quick inspiration, he got her mother's Bible and said: "Now, Gwen, try to see it as I read." But before he read, with a true artist's instinct, he created the proper atmosphere. By a few vivid words he made us feel the pathetic loneliness of the Man of Sorrows in His last sad days. Then he read that masterpiece of all tragedy, the story of Gethsemane. As he read we saw it all. The garden and the trees and the sorrow-stricken Man alone with His mysterious agony. We heard the prayer so pathetically submissive and then, for answer, the crowd and the traitor.

Gwen was far too quick to need explanation, and the Pilot only said, "You see, Gwen, God gave nothing but the best to His own Son, only the best."

"The best? They took Him away, didn't they?" She knew the story well.

"Yes, but listen." He turned the pages rapidly and read: "'We see Jesus for the suffering of death crowned with glory and honor.' That is how He got His kingdom."

Gwen listened silently, but she was unconvinced, and she said, "But how can this be best for me? I am no use to anyone. It can't be best to just lie here and make them all wait on me, and . . . and . . . I did want to help Daddy . . . and . . . oh . . . I know they will get tired of me! They are getting tired already . . . I . . . I . . . can't help being hateful."

She was sobbing by this time as I had never heard her before—deep, passionate sobs. Then again the Pilot had an inspiration.

"Now, Gwen," he said severely, "you know we're not as mean as that, and that you are just talking nonsense, every word. Now I'm going to smooth out your red hair and tell you a story."

"It's *not* red," she cried, between her sobs. This was her sore point.

"It is red as red can be; a beautiful, shining purple *red*," said the Pilot emphatically, beginning to brush.

"Purple!" cried Gwen, scornfully.

"Yes, I've seen it in the sun, purple. Haven't you?" said the Pilot, appealing to me. "And my story is about the canyon, our canyon, your canyon, down there."

"Is it true?" asked Gwen, already soothed by the cool, quick-moving hands.

"True? It's as true as . . . as . . ." he glanced around the room, "as the *Pilgrim's Progress*." This was satisfactory, and the story went on.

"At first there were no canyons, but only the broad, open prairie. One day the Master of the Prairie, walking out over His great lawns, where only grasses grew, asked the Prairie, 'Where are your flowers?' and the Prairie said, 'Master, I have no seeds.' Then the Master spoke to the birds, and they carried seeds of every kind of flower and strewed them far and wide, and soon the Prairie bloomed with crocuses and roses and buffalo beans and yellow crowfoot and wild sunflowers and red lilies.

"Then the Master came and was well pleased, but He missed the flowers He loved best of all, and He said to the Prairie, 'Where are the clematis, the columbine, the sweet violets, windflowers, and all the ferns and flowering shrubs?' Again he spoke to the birds, and again they carried seeds and spread them far and wide.

"But, again, when the Master came, he could not find the flowers he loved best of all, and he said, 'Where are those, my sweetest flowers?' and the Prairie cried sorrowfully, 'Oh, Master, I cannot keep the flowers, for the winds sweep fiercely, and the sun beats down, and they wither and die.' Then the Master spoke to the Lightning, and with one swift blow the Lightning cleft the Prairie to the heart. And the Prairie rocked and groaned in agony and for many days moaned bitterly over its gaping wound. But the Little Swan poured its waters through the cleft and carried down deep black mud, and once more birds carried seeds and spread them in the canyon.

"After a long time, the rocks were decked out with soft mosses and trailing vines, the nooks were hung with clematis, and great elms lifted their huge tops high into the sunlight, while down about their feet clustered the low cedars and balsams, and everywhere violets, windflower, and maidenhair grew and bloomed, till the canyon became the Master's place for rest, peace, and joy."

The quaint tale was ended, and Gwen lay quiet for some moments, then said gently, "Yes! The canyon flowers are the best. Tell me what it means."

Then the Pilot read to her: "'The fruit'—I'll read *flowers*—'of the Spirit are love, joy, peace, longsuffering, gentleness, goodness, faith, meekness, and temperance'—and some of these grow only in the canyon."

"Which are the canyon flowers?" asked Gwen softly.

The Sky Pilot answered, "Gentleness, meekness, and self-control. But though the others, such as love, joy, and peace, bloom in the open, never do they bloom so richly and with so sweet a perfume as in the canyon."

For a long time Gwen lay quite still, and then she said wistfully, while her lip trembled, "There are no flowers in my canyon, only ragged rocks."

"Some day they will bloom, Gwen. He will find them, and we too shall see them."

Then he said good-bye and we left. He had done his work for that day.

To the Duke it was all a wonder, for as the days shortened outside they brightened inside, and Gwen's room gradually became the brightest spot in all the house. The Duke asked the Pilot, "What did you do to the Little Princess, and what's all this about the canyon and its flowers?"

The Pilot told the Duke the same thing he had told Gwen: "The fruit of the Spirit is love, joy, peace, longsuffering, gentleness, goodness, faith, meekness, and temperance—and some of these are found only in the canyon."

The Duke, standing up straight, handsome, and strong, looked back at the Pilot and said, "Do you know, I believe you're right."

"Yes, I'm quite sure," answered the Pilot. "When you come to your canyon, remember."

"When I come!" said the Duke, and a quick spasm of pain passed over his face. "God help me, it's not too far away now." Then he smiled again his old smile and said, "Yes, you are all right, for, of all flowers I have seen, none are fairer or sweeter than those that are waving in Gwen's Canyon."

14

Bill's Bluff

The Pilot had set his heart on building a church in the Swan Creek district, partly because he was human and wished to set a mark of remembrance upon the country, but more because he felt that a congregation must have a home if it is to stay.

All through the summer he kept setting this as a project both desirable and possible to achieve. But few were found to agree with him.

Little Mrs. Muir was one of the few, and she was not one to be disregarded, but her influence was neutralized by the solid immobility of her husband. He had never done anything sudden in his life. Every resolve was the result of a long process of mind, and every act of importance had to be previewed from all possible points. An honest man, strongly religious, and a great admirer of the Pilot, but slow-moving as a glacier, although with plenty of fire in him deep down.

"He's sound at the hairt, ma man Robbie," his wife said to the Pilot, who was fuming and fretting at the blocking of his plans, "but he's terrible deleeberate. Bide ye a bit, laddie. He'll come tae."

"But meantime the summer's going and nothing will be done," was the Pilot's distressed and impatient answer.

So a meeting was called to discuss the question of building a church, with the result that the five men and three women present decided that for the present nothing could be done. This was really Robbie's opinion, though he refused to do or say anything but grunt, as the Pilot, in a rage, said to me afterwards. Williams, the storekeeper, did all the talking, but no one paid much attention to his fluent fatuities except that they represented the unexpressed mind of the dour, exasperating little Scotchman, who sat silent.

The schoolhouse was quite sufficient for the present; the people were too few and too poor, and they were getting on well under the leadership of their present minister. These were the arguments that Robbie's "ay" stamped as quite unanswerable.

It was a sore blow to the Pilot, who had set his heart upon a church. In this saddened state of mind he rode up with me on our weekly visit to the little girl shut up in her lonely house among the hills.

It had become the Pilot's custom during these weeks to turn for cheer to that little room, and seldom was he disappointed. She was so bright, so brave, so full of fun, that gloom faded from her presence as mist before the sun, and impatience was shamed into contentment.

Gwen's bright face—it was almost always bright now—and her cheery welcome did something for the Pilot. Yet the feeling of failure was upon him, and failure to his enthusiastic nature was worse than pain. Not that he confessed to either failure or gloom; he was far too much a man for that, but Gwen felt his depression in spite of all his brave attempts at brightness, and expressed her concern that he might be ill.

"Oh, it's only his church," I said, proceeding to give her an account of Robbie Muir's silent, solid inertness and how he had blocked the Pilot's plan.

"What a shame!" cried Gwen. "What a bad man he must be!"

The Pilot smiled. "No," he answered, "why he's the best man in the place, but I wish he would say or do something. If he would only get mad and swear I think I should feel happier."

Gwen looked quite mystified.

"You see, he sits there in solemn silence looking so tremendously wise that most men feel foolish if they speak. As for his *doing* anything the idea appears preposterous, in the face of his immovableness."

"I can't bear him!" cried Gwen. "I should like to stick pins in him."

"I wish someone would," answered the Pilot. "It would make him seem more human if he could be made to jump."

"Try again," said Gwen, "and get someone to make him jump."

"It would be easier to build the church," said the Pilot, gloomily.

"I could make him jump," said Gwen. "And I *will*," she added.

"You!" answered the Pilot, his eyes widening. "How?"

"I'll find some way," she replied.

And so she did, for when the next meeting was called to discuss the building of a church, the congregation, chiefly of farmers and their wives, with Williams, the storekeeper, were greatly surprised to see Bronco Bill, Hi, and a half-dozen ranchers and cowboys walk in at intervals and solemnly seat themselves. Robbie looked at them with surprise and a little suspicion. In church matters he had no dealings with the Samaritans from the hills. While, in their unregenerate condition, they might be regarded as suitable objects of a missionary effort, their having any part in church policy was to Robbie like casting pearls before swine.

The Pilot, though surprised to see Bill and the cattlemen, was delighted, and he faced the meeting with more confidence. He stated the question up for discussion: "Should a church building be erected this summer in Swan Creek?" And he put his case well, showing the need of a church for the sake of the congregation, for the sake of the men and families in the district, the incoming settlers, and for the sake of the country and its future. He called upon all who loved their church and their country to unite in this effort. It was an enthusiastic appeal, and all the women and some of the men were on his side.

Then followed dead, solemn silence. Robbie was content to wait till the effect of the speech should be dissipated in smaller talk. Then he gravely said, "The kirk wad be a gran' thing, nae doot, an' they wad a' dootless"—with a suspicious glance toward Bill—"rejoice in its construction. But we must be cautious, an' I wad like to enquire hoo much money a kirk cud be built for, and whaur the money wad come frae?"

The Pilot was ready with his answer. The cost would be $1,200. The church-building fund would contribute $200, the people could give $300 in labor, and the remaining $700 he thought could be raised in the district in two years' time.

"Ay," said Robbie, and the tone and manner were sufficient to drench any enthusiasm with the chilliest of water. So much was this the case that the chairman, Williams, seemed quite justified in saying, "It is quite evident that the opinion of the meeting is adverse to any attempt to load the community with a debt of one thousand dollars," and he proceeded with a very complete statement of the many and various objections to any attempt at building a church this year. The people were very few, they were dispersed over a large area, they were not interested sufficiently, and they were all spending money and making little in return. He supposed, therefore, that the meeting might adjourn.

Robbie sat silent and expressionless in spite of his little wife's anxious whispers and nudges. The Pilot looked the picture of woe when suddenly Bill startled the room by speaking: "Say, boys! They haint't much stuck on their religion, heh?" The low, drawling voice was perfectly distinct and arresting.

"Hain't got no use for it, seemingly," was the answer from a dark corner.

"Old Scotchie takes his religion out in prayin', I guess," drawled in Bill, "but wants to sponge for his plant."

This reference to Robbie's proposal to use the school moved the youngsters to tittering and made the little Scotchman squirm, for he prided himself on his independence.

"There ain't $700 in the whole outfit." This was a stranger's voice, and again Robbie squirmed, for he prided himself also on his ability to pay his way.

"No good!" said another emphatic voice. "A lot o' psalm-singing snipes."

"Order, order!" shouted the chairman.

"Old Windbag there don't see any show for swipin' the collection, with Scotchie round," said Hi, with a following ripple of quiet laughter, for Williams's reputation was none too secure.

Robbie was in a most uncomfortable state of mind. So unusually stirred was he that for the first time in his history he made a motion.

"I move we adjourn, Mr. Chairman," he said, in a voice which actually vibrated with emotion.

"Different here! Eh boys?" drawled Bill.

"You bet," said Hi, in huge delight. "The meetin' ain't out yit."

"Ye can bide till mornin'," said Robbie, angrily. "A'm gaen hame," he added, beginning to put on his coat.

"Seems as if he orter give the password," drawled Bill.

"Right you are, pardner," said Hi, springing

to the door and waiting in delighted expectation for his friend's lead.

Robbie looked at the door, then at his wife, and he hesitated a moment, no doubt wishing her home. Then Bill stood up and began to speak.

"Mr. Chairman, I hain't been called on for any remarks."

"Go on!" yelled his friend from the dark corner. "Hear! hear!"

"An' I didn't feel as if this war hardly my game, though the Pilot ain't mean about invitin' a feller on Sunday afternoons. But them as runs the shop don't seem to want us fellers round too much."

Robbie was gazing keenly at Bill, and here shook his head, muttering angrily: "Hoots, nonsense! Ye're welcome inuff."

"But," went on Bill, slowly, "I guess I've been on the wrong track. I've been a cherishin' the opinion" ["Hear! hear!" yelled his admirers], "cherishin' the opinion," repeated Bill, "that these fellers," pointing to Robbie, "was stuck on religion, which I ain't much myself, and reely consarned about blocking of the devil, which the Pilot says can't be did without a regular Gospel factory. O' course, it tain't any biznis of mine, but if us fellers was reely only sot on anything condoocin'," ["Hear! hear!" yelled Hi, in ecstasy], "condoocin,'" repeated Bill more slowly and with relish, "to the good of the Order" (Bill was a brotherhood man), "I b'lieve I know whar five hundred dollars mebbe cud per'aps be got."

"You bet your sox," yelled a strange voice, in chorus with other shouts of approval.

"O' course, I ain't no bettin' man," went on Bill, insinuatingly, "as a regular thing, but I'd gamble a few jist here on this pint; if the boys was stuck on anythin' costin' about seven hundred dollars, it seems to me likely they'd git it in about two days, per'aps."

Here Robbie grunted out an "ay" so full of contemptuous unbelief that Bill paused, and, looking over Robbie's head, he drawled out, even more slowly and mildly, "I ain't much given to bettin', as I remarked before, but, if a man shakes money at me on that proposition, I'd accommodate him to a limited extent." ["Hear! hear! Bully boy!" yelled Hi again.] "Not bein' too bold, I cherish the opinion that even this here Gospel plant, seein' the Pilot's rather sot onto it, I b'lieve the boys could find five hundred dollars inside of a month, if perhaps these fellers cud wiggle the rest out of their pants."

Then Robbie, in great anger and stung by the taunting, drawling voice beyond all self-command broke out suddenly: "Ye'll no can mak that guid, I doot."

"D'ye mean I ain't prepared to back it up?"

"Ay," said Robbie, grimly.

"'Tain't likely I'll be called on; I guess five hundred dollars is safe enough," drawled Bill, cunningly drawing him on. Then Robbie bit.

"Oo ay!" said he, in a voice of quiet contempt, "the twa hunner wull be here and 'twull wait ye long inuff, I'se warrant ye."

Then Bill nailed him.

"I hain't got my card case on my person," he said, with a slight grin.

"Left it on the pianner," suggested Hi, in a state of great hilarity at Bill's success in drawing the Scottie.

"But," Bill proceeded, recovering himself, and with increasing suavity, "if some gentleman would mark down the date, I cherish the opinion that one month from today there will be five hundred dollars lookin' round for two hundred on that there desk mebbe, or p'raps you would incline to two-fifty," he drawled, in his most winning tone to Robbie, who was growing more impatient every moment.

"Nae matter tae me. Ye're haverin' like a daft loon, ony way."

"You will make a memo of this slight transaction, boys, and per'aps the school master will write it down," said Bill.

It was all carefully taken down, and amid much enthusiastic confusion the ranchers and their gang carried Bill off to Old Latour's to "licker up," while Robbie, in deep wrath but dour silence, went off through the dark with his little wife following some paces behind him. His chief grievance, however, was against the chairman for "alooin' sich a disorderly pack o' loons tae disturb respectable fowk," for he could not hide the fact that he had been made to break through his accustomed immovable silence. I suggested, talking with him the next day, that Bill was only baiting. "Ay," said Robbie, in great disgust, "the daft eejut, he wad mak a fule o' onything or onybuddie."

That was the sorest point with poor Robbie. Bill had not only cast doubts upon his religious sincerity, which the little man could not endure, but he had also held him up to the ridicule of the community. But when he understood, some days later, that Bill was taking steps to back up his offer and had been heard to declare that "he'd make them pious ducks take water if he had to put up a year's pay," Robbie went quietly to work to make good his part of the bargain. For his Scotch pride would not suffer him to refuse a challenge from such a quarter.

15

Bill's Partner

The next day everyone was talking of Bill's bluffing the church people, and there was much quiet chuckling over the disconcertment of Robbie Muir and his party.

The Pilot was equally distressed and bewildered, for Bill's conduct, so very unusual, had only one explanation—the usual one for any folly in that country.

"I wish he had waited till after the meeting to go to Latour's. He spoiled the last chance I had. There's no use now," he said.

"But he may do something," I suggested.

"Oh, fiddle!" said the Pilot. "He was only giving Muir 'a song and dance,' as he would say. The whole thing is off."

But when I told Gwen the story of the night's proceedings, she was thrilled to hear of Bill's grave speech and his success in drawing the canny Scotchman.

"Oh, lovely! Dear old Bill and his 'cherished opinion.' Isn't he just lovely? Now he'll do something."

"Who, Bill?"

"No, that stupid Scottie."

"Not he, I'm afraid. Of course Bill was just bluffing him. But it was good sport."

"Oh, lovely! I knew he'd do something."

"Who? Scottie?" I asked, for her pronouns were confusing.

"No!" she cried, "Bill! He promised he would, you know."

"So, you were at the bottom of it?" I said, amazed.

"Oh, dear! Oh, dear!" she kept repeating through shrieks of laughter over Bill's opinions. "I shall be sick. Dear old Bill. He said he'd 'try to get a move on him.'"

Before I left that day, Bill himself came to the Old Timer's ranch, inquiring in a casual way if the "boss" was in.

"Oh, Bill!" called out Gwen, "come in here at once; I want to see you."

After some delay and some shuffling with hat and spurs, Bill lounged in and sat his lank form upon the far end of a bench at the door, trying to look unconcerned as he remarked, "Gittin' cold. Shouldn't wonder if we'd have a little snow."

"Oh, come here," Gwen said, holding out her hand. "Come here and shake hands."

Bill hesitated, spat out his wad of tobacco into a nearby spittoon, and swayed awkwardly across the room toward the bed, and, taking Gwen's hand, he shook it up and down, and hurriedly said, "Fine day, ma'am; hope I see you quite well."

"No, you don't," Gwen answered, laughing, but keeping hold of Bill's hand. "I'm not well a bit, but I'm a great deal better since hearing of your meeting, Bill."

To this Bill made no reply, being entirely engrossed in getting his bony, brown hand out of the grasp of the white, clinging fingers.

"Oh, Bill," went on Gwen, "it was delightful! How did you do it?"

But Bill, who had by this time got back to his seat at the door, pretended ignorance of any achievement needing comment. He "hadn't done nothin' more out of the way than usual."

"Oh, don't talk nonsense!" Gwen rejoined breathlessly. "Tell me how you got Scottie to lay you two hundred and fifty dollars."

"Oh, that!" said Bill, in great surprise, "that ain't nuthin' much."

"But how did you get him?" persisted Gwen. "Tell me, Bill," she added in her most persuasive voice.

"Well" said Bill, "it was easy as rollin' off a log. I made the remark as how the boys ginerally put up for what they wanted without no fuss, and that if they was sot on havin' a Gospel shack, I cherished the opinion . . ." Here Gwen went off into a smothered shriek, which made Bill pause and look at her in alarm.

"Go on," she gasped.

"I cherished the opinion," drawled on Bill, while Gwen stuck her handkerchief into her mouth, "that mebbe they'd put up for it the seven hundred dollars, and, even as it was, seein' as the Pilot appeared to be sot on to it, if them fellers would find two hundred and fifty I cher . . ."

another shriek from Gwen cut him suddenly short.

"It's the rheumaticks, mebbe," said Bill, anxiously. "Terrible bad weather for 'em. I get 'em myself."

"No, no," said Gwen, wiping away her tears and subduing her laughter. "Go on, Bill."

"There ain't no more," said Bill. "He bit, and the master here put it down."

"Yes, it's here right enough," I said, "but I don't suppose you mean to follow it up, do you?"

"You don't, eh? Well, I am not responsible for your supposin', but them that is familiar with Bronco Bill generally expects him to back up his undertakins."

"But how in the world can you get five hundred dollars from the cowboys for a church?"

"I hain't done the arithmetic yet, but it's safe enough. You see, it ain't the church altogether, it's the reputation of the boys."

"I'll help, Bill," said Gwen.

Bill nodded his head slowly and said, "Proud to have you," trying hard to look enthusiastic.

"You don't think I can," said Gwen. Bill protested against the insinuation. "But I can. I'll get Daddy and the Duke too."

"Good line!" said Bill, slapping his knee.

"And I'll give all my money too, but it isn't very much," she added sadly.

"Much!" said Bill, "if the rest of the fellows play up to that lead there won't be any trouble about that five hundred."

Gwen was silent for some time, then said with an air of resolve, "I'll give my pinto!"

"Nonsense!" I exclaimed, while Bill declared "there warn't no call."

"Yes, I'll give the pinto!" said Gwen. "I'll not need him anymore," her lips quivered, and Bill coughed and spat into the bowl, "and besides, I want to give something I like. And Bill will sell him for me!"

"Well," said Bill, slowly, "Now come to think, it'll be purty hard to sell that there pinto." Gwen began to protest, and Bill hurried on to say, "Not but what he ain't a good leetle horse for his weight, good leetle horse, but for cattle . . ."

"Why, Bill, there isn't a better cattle horse anywhere!"

"Yes, that's so," assented Bill. "That's so, if you've got the rider, but put one of them rangers on to him and it wouldn't be no fair show." Bill was growing more convinced by the moment that the pinto wouldn't sell to any advantage. "Ye see," he explained carefully and cunningly, "he ain't a horse you could yank round and slam into a bunch of steers regardless."

Gwen shuddered. "Oh, I wouldn't think of selling him to any of those cowboys." Bill crossed his legs and hitched round uncomfortably on his bench. "I mean one of those rough fellows that don't know how to treat a horse." Bill nodded, looking relieved. "I thought that some one like you, Bill, who knew how to handle a horse . . ."

Gwen paused, and then added, "I'll ask the Duke."

"No call for that," said Bill, "not but what the Duke ain't all right as a jedge of a horse, but the Duke ain't got the connection, it ain't his line." Bill hesitated. "But, if you are real sot on sellin' that pinto, come to think I guess I could find a sale for him, though, of course, I think perhaps the figger won't be high."

And so it was arranged that the pinto should be sold and that Bill would be the one to sell it.

It was characteristic of Gwen that she would not say good-bye to the pony on whose back she had spent so many hours of freedom and delight.

When once she gave him up she refused to allow her heart to cling to him any more.

It was characteristic, too, of Bill that he led the pinto away after night had fallen, so that "his pardner" might be saved the pain of parting.

"This here's rather a new game for me, but when my pardner," here he jerked his head towards Gwen's window, "calls for trumps, I'm blanked if I don't throw my highest, even if it costs a leg."

16

Bill's Financing

Bill's method of conducting the sale of the pinto was eminently successful as a financial operation, but there are those in the Swan Creek country who have never been able to fathom the mystery surrounding the affair. It was at the fall roundup, the beef roundup, as it is called, which this year ended at the Ashley Ranch. There were representatives from all the ranches and some cattlemen from across the line. The hospitality of the Ashley Ranch was up to its own lofty standard, and, after supper, the men were in a state of high exhilaration. The Honorable Fred and his wife, Lady Charlotte, gave themselves to the duties of their position as hosts for the day with heartiness and grace.

After supper the men gathered round the big fire, which was piled up before a long, low, open-fronted shed. Around the fire, most of them wearing "shaps" and all of them wearing wide, hard-brimmed cowboy hats, the men grouped themselves, some reclining on skins thrown about the ground, some standing, smoking, laughing, chatting, all in highest spirits and humor. They had just finished their season of arduous and dangerous work. Their minds were full of the long, hard rides, wild experiences with mad cattle and bucking broncos, and anxious watches through long hot nights, when a breath of wind or a coyote's howl might set the herd off in a frantic stampede. Now these were all behind them. Tonight they were free men and of independent means, for their season's pay was in their pockets.

Bill, as king of the broncobusters, moved about with the slow, careless indifference of a man sure of his position and sure of his ability to maintain it. He spoke seldom and slowly, not as ready-witted as his partner, Hi Kendal, but in act he was swift and sure, and in trouble he could be counted on.

"Hello, Bill," said a friend, "where's Hi? Hain't seen him around."

"Well, I don't jest know. He was going to bring up my pinto."

"Your pinto? What pinto's that? You hain't got no pinto!"

"Mebbe not," said Bill, slowly, "but I had the idee before you spoke that I did."

"That so? Whar'd ye git him? Good for cattle?"

Bill grew mysterious and even more reserved than usual.

"Good fer cattle! Well, I ain't much on gamblin', but I've got a leetle in my pocket that says that there pinto kin outwork any bronco in this outfit, givin' him a fair show after the cattle."

The men became interested.

"Whar was he raised?"

"Dunno."

"Whar'd ye git him? Across the line?"

"No," said Bill stoutly, "right in this here country. The Duke there knows him."

This at once raised the pinto several points. To be known, and, as Bill's tone indicated, favorably known by the Duke, was a testimonial to which any horse might aspire.

"Whar'd ye git him, Bill? Don't be so uncommunicatin'!" said an impatient voice.

Bill hesitated, then, with an apparent burst of confidence, he assumed his frankest manner and voice and told his tale.

"Well," he said, taking a fresh chew and offering his plug to his neighbor, who passed it on after helping himself, "ye see, it was like this. Ye know that little Meredith gel?"

A chorus of voices answered "Yes!"

Bill paused, straightened himself a little, dropped his frank air, and drawled out in cool, hard tones, "I might remark that that young lady is, I might persoom to say, a friend of mine, which I'm prepared to back up in my best style, and if any son of a street sweeper has any remark to make, here's his time now!"

In the pause that followed, murmurs were heard extolling the many excellences of the young lady in question, and Bill, appeased, continued his story by describing Gwen and her pinto and her work on the ranch. The men, many of whom had had glimpses of her, gave emphatic approval in their own way. But as he told of her rescue of

BILL'S FINANCING

Joe and of the sudden calamity that had befallen her, a great stillness fell upon the simple, tender-hearted fellows, and they listened with their eyes shining in the firelight with growing intentness. Then Bill spoke of the Pilot and how he stood by her and helped her and cheered her till they began to swear he was "all right." "And now," Bill concluded, "when the Pilot is in a hole she wants to help him out."

"O' course," said one. "Right enough. How's she going to work it?" said another.

"Well, he's dead set on buildin' a meetin' house, and them fellows down at the Creek that does the prayin' and such don't seem to back him up!"

"Whar's the kick, Bill?"

"Oh, they don't want to go down into their pockets and put up for it."

"How much?"

"Why, he only asked 'em for seven hundred for the hull outfit, and would give 'em two years, but they bucked—wouldn't look at it."

At this, the group as one muttered in expletives descriptive of the character and personal appearance of the congregation down at Swan Creek.

"Were you there, Bill? What did you do?"

"Oh," said Bill, "I didn't do much. Gave 'em a little bluff."

"No! How? What? Go on, Bill."

But Bill remained silent, till under stronger pressure, and, as if making a clean breast of everything, said, "Well, I jest told 'em that if you boys made such a fuss about anythin' like they did about their Gospel outfit, an' I ain't sayin' anythin' agin it, you'd put up seven hundred without turnin' a hair."

"You're the stuff, Bill! Good man! You're talkin' now! What did they say to that, eh, Bill?"

"Well," said Bill, slowly, "they *called* me!"

"No! That so? An' what did you do, Bill?"

"Gave 'em a dead straight bluff!"

After the shouts of approval died down, another voice asked, "Did they take you, Bill?"

"Well, I reckon they did. The master, here, put it down."

Whereupon I read the terms of Bill's bluff.

There was a chorus of very hearty approvals of Bill's course in "not taking any water" from that "outfit." But the responsibility of the situation began to dawn upon them when someone asked, "How are you going about it, Bill?"

"Well," drawled Bill, with a touch of sarcasm in his voice, "there's that pinto."

"Pinto!" said young Hill. "Say, boys, is that little girl going to lose that one pony of hers to help out her friend the Pilot? Good fellow, too, he is! We know he's the right sort."

"Then," went on Bill, even more slowly, "there's the Pilot: he's going to ante up a month's pay—'taint much, o' course—twenty-eight a month and grub himself. Twenty-eight a month and grub himself o' course ain't much for a man to save money out of to eddicate himself." Bill continued, as if thinking aloud, "O' course he's got his mother at home, but she can't make much more than her own livin', but she might help him some."

This was altogether too much for the crowd and they hooted in derision at the plans Bill had laid out for raising the needed amount.

"O' course," Bill explained, "it's jest as you boys feel about it. Mebbe I was bein' hot, a little swift in givin' 'em the bluff."

"Not much, you wasn't! We'll see you out! That's the talk! There's between twenty and thirty of us here."

"I should be glad to contribute thirty or forty

if need be," said the Duke, who was standing not far off, "to assist in the building of a church. It would be a good thing, and I think the parson should be encouraged. He's the right sort."

"I'll cover your thirty," said young Hill; and so it went from one to another in tens and fifteens and twenties, till within half an hour I had entered three hundred and fifty dollars in my book, with Ashley yet to hear from, which meant fifty more. It was Bill's hour of triumph.

"Boys," he said, "ye're all right. But that leetle pale-faced gel, that's what I'm thinkin' on. Won't she open them big eyes of hers! I cherish the opinion that this'll tickle her some."

The men were greatly pleased with Bill and even more pleased with themselves. Bill's picture of the "leetle gel" and her pathetically tragic lot had gone right to their hearts, and with men of that mold it was one of their few luxuries to yield to generous impulses. Most of them had few opportunities of lavishing love and sympathy on worthy objects, and when the opportunity came, all that was best in them clamored for expression.

17

How the Pinto Sold

The men had just begun to arrange themselves in groups around the fire for poker and other games when Hi rode up into the light and with him a stranger on Gwen's beautiful pinto pony.

Hi was evidently half drunk and, as he swung himself off his bronco, he saluted the company with a wave of the hand.

Bill, looking curiously at Hi, went up to the pinto and taking him by the head, led him up into the light, saying, "See here, boys, there's that pinto of mine I was telling you about; no flies on him, eh?"

"Hold on there! Excuse me!" said the stranger, "this here hoss belongs to me, if paid-down money means anything in this country."

"The country's all right," said Bill in an ominously quiet voice, "but this here pinto's another transaction, I reckon."

"The hoss is mine, I say, and what's more, I'm goin' to hold him," said the stranger in a loud voice.

The men began to crowd around with faces growing hard. It was dangerous in that country to play fast and loose with horses.

"Look a hyar, mates," said the stranger, with a Yankee drawl, "I ain't no hoss thief, and if I hain't bought this hoss reg'lar and paid down good money then it ain't mine—if I have, it is. That's fair, ain't it?"

At this Hi pulled himself together, and in a half-drunken tone declared that the stranger was all right and that he had bought the horse fair and square. "And there's your dust," said Hi, handing a roll to Bill. But with a quick movement Bill caught the stranger by the leg, and before a word could be said, the stranger was lying flat on the ground.

"You git off that pony," Bill demanded, "till this thing is settled."

There was something so terrible in Bill's manner that the man contented himself with blustering and swearing, while Bill, turning to Hi, said, "Did you sell this pinto to him?"

Hi acknowledged that, being offered a good price and knowing that his partner was always ready for a deal, he had transferred the pinto to the stranger for forty dollars.

Bill was in deep distress and explained, "tain't the horse, but the leetle gel." But his partner's deal was his, and angry as he was, he refused to attempt to break the bargain.

At this moment the Honorable Fred, noting the unusual excitement about the fire came up, followed at a little distance by his wife and the Duke.

"Perhaps he'll sell," he suggested.

"No," said Bill sullenly, "he's a mean cuss."

"I know him," said the Honorable Fred, "let me try." But the stranger declared the pinto suited him and he wouldn't take twice his money for him.

"Why," he protested, "that there's what I call an unusual hoss, and down in Montana for a lady he'd fetch up to a hundred and fifty dollars." They haggled and bargained in vain; the man was immovable. Eighty dollars he wouldn't look at, a hundred hardly made him hesitate.

At this point Lady Charlotte came down into the light and stood by her husband, who explained the circumstances to her. She had already heard Bill's description of Gwen's accident and of her part in the church-building schemes. There was silence for a few moments as she stood looking at the beautiful pony.

"What a shame the poor child should have to part with the dear little creature," she said in a low tone to her husband. Then, turning to the stranger, she said in clear, sweet tones, "What do you ask for him?"

The stranger hesitated and then said, lifting his hat awkwardly in salute, "I was just remarking how that pinto would fetch one hundred and fifty dollars down into Montana. But seein' as a lady is enquirin', I'll put him down to one hundred and twenty-five."

"Too much," she said promptly, "far too much, is it not, Bill?"

"Well," drawled Bill, "if 'twere a fellar as was used to ladies, he'd offer you the pinto, but he's too mean even to come down to the even hundred."

The Yankee took him up quickly. "Wall, if I were so—pardon, madam," taking off his hat, "used to ladies as some folks would like to think themselves, I'd buy that there pinto and make a present of it to this here lady as stands before me."

Bill twisted uneasily.

The stranger continued: "But I ain't goin' to be mean; I'll put that pinto in for the even money for the lady if any man cares to put up the stuff."

"Well, my dear," said the Honorable Fred with a bow, "we cannot let that challenge lie." She turned and smiled at him and the pinto was transferred to the Ashley stables, to Bill's outspoken delight in declaring that he "couldn't have faced the music if that there pinto had gone across the line."

I confess, however, I was somewhat surprised at the ease with which Hi escaped his wrath, and my surprise was in no way lessened when I saw, later in the evening, the two partners with the stranger taking a quiet drink out of the same bottle with evident mutual admiration and delight.

"You're an A-one corker, you are! I'll be hornswoggled if you ain't a bird—a singin' bird—a reg'lar canary," I heard Hi say to Bill.

But Bill's only reply was a long, slow wink that passed into a frown as he caught my eye. My suspicion was aroused, and the sale of the pinto might bear some investigation. This suspicion was deepened when the next week Gwen gave me a rapturous account of how splendidly Bill had disposed of the pinto, showing me bills for one hundred and fifty dollars! To my look of amazement, Gwen replied, "You see, he must have got them bidding against each other, and besides, Bill says pintos are going up."

Light began to dawn on me, but I only answered that I knew they had risen considerably in value within a month. The extra fifty was Bill's.

I was not present to witness the finishing of Bill's bluff, but I was told that when Bill made his way through the crowded aisle and laid his five hundred and fifty dollars on the schoolhouse desk, the look of disgust, surprise, and finally of pleasure on Robbie's face was worth a hundred more. But Robbie was ready and put down his two hundred with the single remark: "Ay! Ye're no as daft as ye look," mid roars of laughter from all.

Then the Pilot, with eyes and face shining, rose and thanked them all. But when he told of how the little girl in her lonely shack in the hills thought so much of the church that she gave up her beloved pony, her one possession, the light from his eyes was reflected into the eyes of all.

The men from the ranches, who could understand the full meaning of her sacrifice and who also could realize the full measure of her calamity, were stirred to the depths of their hearts. And when Bill remarked in a very distinct undertone, "I cherish the opinion that this here Gospel shop wouldn't be materializin' into its present shape but for thet leetle gel," there rose growls of approval, leaving no doubt that his opinion was that of all.

Though the Pilot never could quite get at the true secret of Bill's methods, and while Gwen was responsible for the spring to action, he knew in his heart that Bill's bluff had a great deal to do with the "materializin'" of the first church in Swan Creek.

Whether the Honorable Fred ever understood the peculiar style of Bill's financing, I do not quite know. But if he ever did come to know, he was far too much of a man to make a fuss. Besides, I fancy the smile on his lady's face was worth some large amount to him; at least, so the look of proud and fond love in his eyes seemed to say as he turned away with her from the fire the night of the pinto's sale.

18

The Lady Charlotte

The night of the pinto's sale was a momentous night for Gwen, for it was that night that the Lady Charlotte's interest in her began. It was momentous, too, for the Lady Charlotte, for it was that night that brought the Pilot into her life.

I had turned back to the fire around which the men had grouped themselves, and was ready for an hour's solid delight, for the scene was full of wild and picturesque beauty, when the Duke came and touched my shoulder.

"Lady Charlotte would like to see you."

"And why?" I asked.

"She wants to hear about this affair of Bill's."

We went through the kitchen into the large dining room, at one end of which was a stone chimney and fireplace. Lady Charlotte had declared that she did not much care what kind of a house the Honorable Fred would build for her, but that she must have a fireplace.

There was a reserve and a grand air in her bearing that put people in awe of her. I shared the awe, but as I entered the room she welcomed me with such kindly grace that I felt quite at ease. She was very beautiful—tall, slight, and graceful in every line.

"Come and sit by me," she invited, drawing an armchair into the circle about the fire. "I want you to tell us about a great many things."

"You see what you're in for," said her husband. "It is a serious business when my lady takes one in hand."

"As he well knows," she said, smiling and shaking her head at her husband.

She turned back and said to me, "Now, tell me first about Bill's encounter with that funny little Scotchman."

I told her the account of Bill's bluff in my

best style, imitating, as I have some small skill in doing, the manner and speech of the various participants in the story. She was greatly amused and interested.

"And Bill has really got his share ready," she exclaimed. "It is very clever of him."

"Yes," I replied, "but Bill is only the very humble instrument; the moving spirit is behind."

"Oh, yes, you mean the little girl who owns the pony," she said. "That's another thing you must tell me about."

"The Duke knows more than I," I replied, shifting the burden to him. "My acquaintance seems only of yesterday; his is lifelong."

"Why have you never told me of her?" she demanded, turning to the Duke.

"Haven't I told you of the little Meredith girl? Surely I have," said the Duke, sounding not so sure of himself.

"Now, you know quite well you have not, and that means you are deeply interested. Oh, I know you well," she said severely.

"He is the most secretive man," she went on to me, "shamefully reserved."

The Duke smiled, then lazily said, "Why, she's just a child. Why should you be interested in her?

No one was," he added sadly, "till misfortune distinguished her."

Her eyes grew soft, and her gay manner changed, and she said to the Duke: "Tell me of her now."

It was evidently an effort, but he began his story of Gwen from the time he saw her first, years ago, playing in and out of her father's rambling shack, shy and wild as a young fox. As he went on with his tale, his voice dropped to a low, musical tone, and he seemed as if dreaming aloud. Unconsciously he put into the tale much of himself, revealing how great an influence the little child had had upon him and how empty of love his life had been in this lonely land. Lady Charlotte listened with face intent upon him, and even her bluff husband was conscious that something more than usual was happening. He had never heard the Duke break through his proud reserve before.

But when the Duke graphically told the story of Gwen's awful fall, a little red spot burned on the Lady Charlotte's pale cheek, and as the Duke finished with the words "It was her last ride," she covered her face with her hands and cried.

Lady Charlotte at last looked up from her

hands: "Oh, Duke, it is horrible to think of! But what splendid courage! How is she now?"

The Duke looked up as from a dream. "Bright as the morning," he said. Then, in reply to Lady Charlotte's look of wonder, he added, "the Pilot did it. The schoolmaster will tell you. I don't understand it."

"Nor do I," I quickly responded, "but I can tell you only what I saw and heard."

"Tell me," said the Lady Charlotte very gently.

Then I told her how, one by one, we had failed to help, and how the Pilot had ridden up that morning through the canyon and how he had brought the first light and peace to her by his marvelous pictures of the flowers, ferns, trees, and all the wonderful mysteries of that place.

"But that wasn't all," said the Duke.

"No," I said slowly, "that was *not* all by a long shot—but the rest I don't understand. That's the Pilot's secret."

"Tell me what he did," said the Lady Charlotte, softly once more. "I want to know."

"I don't think I can," I replied. "He simply read out of the Scriptures to her and talked."

Lady Charlotte looked disappointed. "Is that all?"

"It is quite enough for Gwen," answered the Duke, "for there she lies, often suffering, always longing for the hills and the free air, but with her face radiant as the flowers of her beloved canyon."

"I must see her," decided the Lady Charlotte aloud, "and that wonderful Pilot too."

"You'll be disappointed in him," said the Duke.

"Oh, I've seen him and heard him, but I don't know him," she responded. "There must be something in him that one does not see at first."

"So I have discovered," said the Duke, and with that the subject was dropped, but not before the Lady Charlotte made me promise to take her to Gwen, the Duke being strangely unwilling to do this for her.

Again he warned, "You'll be disappointed. She is only a simple little child."

But Lady Charlotte thought differently, and, having made up her mind upon the matter, there was nothing to do as her husband said but "for all hands to surrender and the sooner the better."

And so the Lady Charlotte had her way, which, as it turned out was much the wisest and best.

19

Through Gwen's Window

When I told the Pilot of Lady Charlotte's intention to visit Gwen, he was not pleased.

"What does she want with Gwen?" he asked impatiently. "She will just put notions into her head and make her discontented."

"Why should she?" I replied.

"She won't mean to, but she belongs to another world, and Gwen cannot talk to her without getting glimpses of a life that will make her long for what she can never have," he responded.

"But suppose it is not idle curiosity in Lady Charlotte," I suggested.

"I don't say it is that," he answered, "but these people love a sensation."

"I don't think you know Lady Charlotte," I replied. "I hardly think from her tone the other night that she is a sensation hunter."

"At any rate," he answered, "she is not to worry poor Gwen."

I was a little surprised at his attitude, and felt that he was unfair to Lady Charlotte, but I didn't want to argue with him. He could not bear to think of any person or thing threatening the peace of his beloved Gwen.

The very first Saturday after my promise was given we were surprised to see Lady Charlotte ride up to the door of our shack in the early morning.

"You see I am not going to let you off," she said as I greeted her. "And the day is so very fine for a ride."

I hastened to apologize for not going to her, and then to get out of my difficulty, rather meanly turned toward the Pilot, and said, "The Pilot doesn't approve of our visit."

"And why not, may I ask?" said Lady Charlotte, lifting her eyebrows.

The Pilot's face burned, partly with wrath at me and partly with embarrassment, for Lady Charlotte had put on her grand air. But he stood to his guns.

"I was saying, Lady Charlotte," he said, looking straight into her eyes, "that you and Gwen have little in common . . . and . . . and . . . ," he hesitated.

"Little in common!" she responded. "She has suffered greatly."

The Pilot was quick to catch the note of sadness in her voice.

"Yes," he said, wondering at her tone, "she has suffered greatly."

"And," continued Lady Charlotte, "she is bright as the morning, the Duke says." There was a look of pain in her face.

The Pilot's face lit up, and he came nearer and stroked her beautiful horse. "Yes, thank God!" he said, "bright as the morning."

"How can that be?" she asked, looking down into his face. "Perhaps you can tell me."

"Lady Charlotte," said the Pilot with a sudden flush, "I must ask your pardon. I was wrong. I thought you . . . ," he paused. "Go to Gwen; she will tell you. And you will do her good."

"Thank you," said Lady Charlotte, putting out her hand, "and perhaps you will come and see me too."

The Pilot promised and stood looking after us as we rode up the trail.

"There is something more in your Pilot than at first appears," she said. "The Duke was quite right."

"He is a great man," I said with enthusiasm, "tender in spirit but with the heart of a hero."

"You and Bill and the Duke seem to agree about him," she said, smiling.

The I told her tales of the Pilot and of his ways with the men, till her blue eyes grew bright and her beautiful face lost its proud look.

"It is perfectly amazing," I said, finishing my story, "how these devil-may-care, rough fellows respect him and come to him in all sorts of trouble. I can't understand it, and yet he is just a boy."

"No, not amazing," said Lady Charlotte slowly. "I think I understand it. He has a true man's heart, and holds a great purpose in it. I've seen men like that. Not clergymen, I mean, but men with a great purpose."

Then, after a moment's thought, she added,

"But you ought to care for him better. He does not look strong."

"Strong!" I exclaimed, with a strange feeling of resentment. "He can do as much riding as any of us."

"Still, there is something in his face that would make his mother anxious." In spite of my repudiation of her suggestion, I found myself for the next few minutes thinking of how he would come home exhausted and faint from his long rides, and I resolved that he must have a rest and some change.

It was one of those early September days—the best time of year in the western country, when the light falls less fiercely through a soft haze that seems to fill the air about you. By the time we reached the canyon, the sun was riding high and pouring its rays into all the deep nooks.

The tops of the elms were dry and rust-colored, and the poplars and delicate birches were painted in pale yellow and orange. Here and there the sumacs made great splashes of brilliant crimson. We stood some moments silently gazing into this tangle of interlacing boughs and shimmering leaves, then Lady Charlotte broke the silence in tones soft and reverent as if she stood in a great cathedral.

"And this is Gwen's canyon!"

"Yes, but she never sees it now," I said, for I could never ride through without thinking of the child to whose heart this was so dear but whose eyes could never see it. Lady Charlotte made no reply, and we continued on the trail while leaves fluttered down on us from the trees above. The flowers were all gone, but the Little Swan sang as ever as it flowed in pools and cascades with here and there a golden leaf upon its black waters.

As we began to climb up into the open I glanced at my companion's face. The canyon had done its work with her as with all who loved it. The touch of pride that was the habit of her face was gone, and in its place rested the earnest wonder of a little child. And with this face she looked in on Gwen.

And Gwen, who had been waiting for her, forgot all her nervous fear, and with hands outstretched, sang out in welcome:

"Oh, I'm so glad! You've seen it and I know you love it! My canyon, you know!" she went on, answering Lady Charlotte's mystified look.

"Yes, dear child," said Lady Charlotte, bending over the pale face with its halo of golden hair, "I love it." But she could get no further, for her eyes were full of tears.

Gwen gazed up into the beautiful face, wondering at her silence, and then said, "Tell me how it looks today! The Pilot always shows it to me. Do you know," she added thoughtfully, "the Pilot looks like it himself. He makes me think of it, and . . . and," she went on shyly, "you do too."

By this time Lady Charlotte was kneeling by the couch, smoothing the beautiful hair and gently touching the face so pale and lined with pain.

"That is a great honor, truly," she said through her tears, "to be like your canyon and like your Pilot too."

Gwen nodded, but she was not to be denied.

"Tell me how it looks today," she said. "I want to see it. Oh, I want to see it!"

Lady Charlotte was greatly moved by the longing in the voice, but, controlling herself, she smiled and said, "Oh, I can't show it to you as your Pilot can, but I'll tell you what I saw."

"Turn me where I can see," Gwen asked me, and I wheeled her toward the window and raised her up so that she could look down the trail toward the canyon's mouth.

"Now," she said, after the pain of the lifting had passed, "tell me, please."

Then Lady Charlotte set the canyon before her in rich and radiant coloring, while Gwen listened, gazing down on the trail to where the rusty elm tops could be seen.

"Oh, it is lovely!" said Gwen, "and I see it so well. It is all there before me when I look through my window."

But Lady Charlotte looked at her, wondering to see her bright smile, and at last she could not help the question: "But don't you want to see it with your own eyes?"

"Yes," Gwen answered gently. "Often I want and want it, oh, so much!"

"And then, Gwen, dear, how can you bear it?" Her voice was eager and earnest. "Tell me, Gwen. I have heard all about your canyon flowers, but I can't understand how the fretting and the pain went away."

Gwen looked at her first in amazement and then in dawning understanding.

"Have you a canyon too?" she asked.

Lady Charlotte paused a moment, then nodded. It did appear strange to me that she should break down her proud reserve and open her heart to this child.

"And there are no flowers, Gwen, not one," she said rather bitterly, "nor sun nor seeds nor soil, I fear."

"Oh, if the Pilot were here, he would tell you."

At this point, feeling that they would rather be alone, I excused myself on the pretext of looking after the horses.

What they talked about during the next hour I never knew, but when I returned to the room Lady Charlotte was reading aloud and with a perplexed expression out of Gwen's mother's Bible the words "for the suffering of death, crowned with glory and honor."

"You see even for Him—suffering," Gwen said eagerly, "but I can't explain. The Pilot will make it clear." Then the talk ended.

We had lunch with Gwen—bannocks and fresh sweet milk and blueberries—and after an hour of lively fun we departed.

Lady Charlotte kissed her tenderly as she said good-bye.

"You must let me come again and sit at your

window," she said, smiling down upon the wan face.

"Oh, I shall watch for you. How good that will be!" Gwen said with delight. "How many come to see me! You make five." Then she softly added, "You will write your letter."

But Lady Charlotte shook her head. "I can't do that, I fear," she said, "but I will think about it."

It was a bright face that peered at us through the open window as we rode down the trail. Just before we took the dip into the canyon, I turned to wave my hand.

"Gwen's friends always wave from here," I said, wheeling my bronco.

Again and again Lady Charlotte waved her handkerchief.

"How beautiful, but how wonderful!" she said as if to herself. "Truly, *her* canyon is full of flowers."

"It is quite beyond me," I replied. "The Pilot may explain."

"Is there anything your Pilot can't do?" she asked.

"Try him," I ventured.

"I mean to, but I cannot bring anyone to my canyon, I fear," she added in an uncertain voice.

As I left her at her door she thanked me with courteous grace.

"You have done a great deal for me," she said, giving me her hand. "It has been a beautiful day, a wonderful day."

When I told the Pilot all the day's doings, he burst out, "What a stupid and self-righteous fool I have been! I never thought there could be any canyon in her life. How short our sight is!" And all that night I could get almost no words out of him.

That was the first of many visits to Gwen. Not a week passed but Lady Charlotte took the trail to the Meredith ranch and spent an hour at Gwen's window. Often the Pilot found her there. But though they were always pleasant hours to him, he would come home in great trouble about Lady Charlotte.

"She is perfectly charming and doing Gwen no end of good, but she is proud as an archangel. She has had an awful break with her family at home, and it is spoiling her life. She told me so much, but she will allow no one to help."

But one day we met her riding toward the

village. As we drew near, she stopped her horse and held up a letter.

"Home!" she said. "I wrote it today, and I must get it off immediately."

The Pilot understood her at once. "Good!" was his only reply, but he said it with such emphasis that we both laughed.

"Yes, I hope so," she said, with the red beginning to show in her cheeks. "I have dropped some seed into my canyon."

"I think I see the flowers beginning to sprout," said the Pilot.

She shook her head doubtfully and replied, "I shall ride up and sit with Gwen at her window."

"Do," replied the Pilot, "the light is good there. Wonderful things are to be seen through Gwen's window."

"Yes," said Lady Charlotte softly. "Dear Gwen! But I fear it is often made bright with tears."

As she spoke she wheeled her horse and cantered off, for her own tears were not far away.

20

How Bill Favored "Home-Grown Industries"

The building of the Swan Creek Church made a sensation in the country, and all the more so as it was Bronco Bill that was in command.

"When I put up money I stay with the game," he announced. And stay he did, to the great benefit of the work and to the delight of the Pilot, who was wearing himself out in trying to do several men's work.

It was Bill that organized the gangs for hauling stone for the foundation and logs for the walls. It was Bill that assigned the various jobs to those volunteering service. To Robbie Muir and two stalwart Glengarry men from the Ottawa lumber region who knew all about the broadax, he gave the job of hewing down logs that formed the walls. And when they had finished, Bill declared they were "better 'an a sawmill." It was Bill, too, that did the financing, and his negotiations with Williams, the storekeeper from "the other side," who dealt in lumber and building materials, were such that established forever Bill's reputation in finance.

With the Pilot's plans in his hands he went to Williams, seizing a time when the store was full of the men after their mail.

"What do you think of them plans?" he asked innocently.

Williams was fluent with opinions and criticism and suggestions, all of which were gratefully, even humbly, received.

"Kind of hart to figger out jest how much lumber'll go into the shack," said Bill. "Ye see the logs makes a difference."

To Williams the thing was simplicity itself, and, after some figuring, he handed Bill a complete statement of the amount of lumber of all kinds that would be required.

"Now, what would that there come to?"

Williams named his figure, and then Bill entered upon negotiations.

"I ain't no man to beat down prices. No sir, I say give a man his figger. Of course, this here ain't my funeral; besides, bein' a Gospel shop, the price naterally would be different." To this the boys all assented and Williams looked uncomfortable.

"In fact," said Bill, adopting his public tone to Hi's admiration and joy, "this here's a public institooshun" (this was Williams's own thunder), "condoocin' to the good of the community" (Hi slapped his thigh and spat tobacco juice halfway across the store to signify his approval), "and I cherish the opinion that public men are interested in this concern."

"That's so! Right you are!" chorused the boys.

Williams agreed but declared he had thought of all this in making his calculation. But seeing it was a church, and the first church and their own church, he would make a cut, which he did after more figuring. Bill gravely took the slip of paper and put it into his pocket without a word. By the end of the week, having in the meantime ridden into town and interviewed the dealers there, Bill sauntered into the store and took up a position distant from Williams.

"You'll be wanting that sheeting next week, won't you, Bill?" said Williams.

"What sheetin's that?"

"Why, for the church. Ain't the logs up?"

"Yes, that's so. I was just goin' to see the boys here about gettin' it hauled," said Bill.

"Hauled!" said Williams, in amazed indignation. "Ain't you goin' to stick to your deal?"

"I generally make it my custom to stick to my deals," said Bill, looking straight at Williams.

"Well, what about your deal with me last Monday night?" retorted the angry Williams.

"Let's see. Last Monday night," said Bill, apparently thinking back, "can't say as I remember any pertickler deal. Any of you fellers remember?"

No one could recall any deal.

"You don't remember getting any paper from me, I suppose?" Williams said sarcastically.

"Paper! Why, I believe I've got that there paper onto my person at this present moment," said Bill, diving into his pocket and drawing out Williams's estimate. He spent a few moments in careful scrutiny.

"There ain't no deal onto this as I can see," said Bill, passing the paper to the boys, who each scrutinized it and passed it on with a shake of the head or remark as to the absence of any sign of a deal. Williams changed his tone.

Then Bill made him an offer. "Of course, I believe in supportin' home-grown industries, and if you can touch my figger I'd be uncommonly glad to give you the contract."

But Bill's figure, which was almost 50 percent lower than Williams's best offer, was rejected as quite impossible.

"Thought I'd make you the offer," said Bill, carelessly, "seein' as you're institootin' the trade and the boys here'll all be buildin' more or less, and I believe in standin' up for local trades and manufacturers." There were nods of approval on all sides, and Williams was forced to accept, for Bill began arranging with the Hill brothers and Hi to make an early start on Monday. It was a great triumph, but Bill displayed no sign of elation; he was rather full of sympathy for Williams, and eager to help on the lumber business as a local "institooshun."

Second in command in the church building enterprise was Lady Charlotte, and under her labored the Honorable Fred, the Duke, and all the Company of the Noble Seven. Lady Charlotte's home became the center of a new type of social life. With exquisite tact, and much was needed for this kind of work, she drew the bachelors from their lonely shacks and from their wild carousals, and gave them a taste of the joys of a pure home life, the first they had had since leaving the old homes years ago. And then she made them work for the church with such zeal and diligence that her husband and the Duke declared that ranching had become an incidental interest since the church-building had begun.

With such energy did Bill push the work of construction that by the first of December the church stood roofed, sheeted, floored, and ready for windows, doors, and ceiling. The Pilot began to believe that he should see the desire of his heart fulfilled—the church of Swan Creek open for divine service on Christmas Day.

During these weeks there was more than church-building going on, for while the days were given to the shaping of logs, the driving of nails, and the planing of boards, the long winter evenings were spent in talk around the fire in my shack. The Pilot for some months past had made his home with me. And Bill, since the beginning of the church building, had come "to camp." I remember those as great nights, when the Pilot, Bill, and the other boys, after a day's work on the church, would gather together.

We would eat our bacon, beans, and bannocks, and occasionally potatoes or a rare pudding, and we'd wash it all down with rich and steaming coffee. The lighting of pipes would follow, and then yarns of adventures were spun—possible and impossible tales, all exciting and wonderful, and all received with the greatest credulity.

If, however, the powers of belief were put to too great a strain by a tale of more than ordinary marvel, Bill would follow with one of such utter impossibility that the company would feel the limit had been reached, and the yarns would stop. But after the first week, most of the time was given to the Pilot, who would read to us of the deeds of the mighty men of old, who had made and wrecked empires.

What happy nights they were to those cowboys, who had been cast up like driftwood on this strange and lonely shore. Some of them had never known what it was to have a thought beyond the work and sport of the day. And the world into which the Pilot was ushering them was new and wonderful. Those were happy, carefree nights.

21

How Bill Hit the Trail

When "the crowd" was with us, the Pilot read us all sorts of tales of adventures in all lands by heroes of all ages, but when we three sat together by our fire, the Pilot would always read us tales of the heroes of sacred stories, and these delighted Bill more than those of any ancient empires. Bill had his favorites. Abraham, Moses, Joshua, and Gideon never failed to arouse his admiration. But Jacob was to him always "a mean cuss," and David he could not appreciate. Most of all he admired Moses and the apostle

Paul, whom he called "that little chap." But, when the reading was about the One Great Man that moved majestic amid the gospel stories, Bill made no comments; He was too high for approval.

By and by Bill began to tell these tales to the boys, and one night, when a quiet mood had fallen upon the company, Bill broke the silence.

"Say, Pilot, where was it that the little chap got mixed up into that riot?"

"Riot!" said the Pilot.

"Yes, you remember when he stood off the whole gang from the stairs?"

"Oh, yes, at Jerusalem!"

"Yes, that's the spot. Perhaps you would read that to the boys. Good yarn! Little chap, you know, stood up and told 'em they were all sorts of thieves and cutthroats, and he stood 'em off. Played it alone too."

Most of the boys failed to recognize the story in its new dress. There was much interest.

"Who was the duck? Who was the gang? What was the row about?"

"The Pilot here'll tell you. If you'd kind o' give 'em a lead before you begin, they'd catch on to the yarn better," he added to the Pilot who was preparing to read.

"Well, it was at Jerusalem," began the Pilot, when Bill interrupted:

"If I might remark, perhaps it might help the boys on to the trail mebbe, if you'd tell 'em how the little chap struck his new gait." This was Bill's way of describing the apostle's conversion.

Then the Pilot introduced the apostle with some formality to the company, describing with such vivid touches his life and early training, his sudden wrench from all he held dear, his new conviction, his magnificent enthusiasm and courage, and his tenderness and patience. I was surprised to find myself regarding him as a sort of hero, and the boys were all ready to back him against any odds. As the Pilot read the story of the arrest at Jerusalem, stopping now and then to picture the scene, we saw it all and were in the thick of it. The raging crowd hustling and beating the life out of the brave little man, the sudden thrust of the disciplined Roman guard through the mass, the rescue, the pause on the stairway, the calm face of the little hero beckoning for a hearing, the quieting of the frantic, frothing mob, the fearless speech—all passed before us. The boys were thrilled.

"Good stuff, eh?"

"Ain't he a daisy?"

"Daisy! He's a whole sunflower patch!"

"Yes," drawled Bill, highly appreciating their marks of approval. "That's what I call a partickler fine character of a man."

"You bet!" said Hi.

"I say," broke in one of the boys, who was just emerging from the tenderfoot stage, "o' course that's in the Bible, ain't it?"

The Pilot assented.

"Well, how do you know it's true?"

The Pilot was proceeding to explain when Bill cut in somewhat more abruptly than usual.

"Look here, young feller!" Bill's voice was in the tone of command. The young man looked as if he was bid in a game of poker. "How do you know anythin's true? How do you know the Pilot here's true when he speaks? Can't you tell by the feel? You know by the sound of his voice, don't you?" Bill paused and the young fellow readily agreed.

"Well, how do you know a son of an old mule when you see him?" Again Bill paused, and there was no reply.

"Well," said Bill, resuming his deliberate drawl, "I'll give you the information without extra charge. It's by the sound he makes when he opens his jaw." He swore.

"But," went on the young skeptic, nettled at the laugh that went round, "that don't prove anything. You know," turning to the Pilot, "that there are heaps of people who don't believe the Bible."

The Pilot nodded.

"Some of the smartest, best-educated men are agnostics," proceeded the young man, warming to his theme, and failing to notice the stiffening of Bill's lank figure. "I don't know but what I am one myself."

"That so?" said Bill.

"I guess so," was the modest reply.

"Got it bad?" went on Bill, with a note of anxiety in his tone.

But the young man turned to the Pilot and tried to open a fresh argument.

"Whatever he's got," said Bill to the others, in a mild voice, "it's spoilin' his manners."

"Yes," went on Bill, meditatively, after the slight laugh had died, "it's ruinin' to the judgment. He don't seem to know when he interferes with the game. Pity too."

Still the argument went on.

"Seems as if he ought to take somethin'," said Bill, in a voice now suspiciously mild. "What would you suggest?"

"A walk, mebbe!" said Hi, in delighted expectation.

"I hold the opinion that you have mentioned an uncommonly vallable remedy."

Bill rose languidly.

"I say," he drawled, tapping the young fellow, "it appears to me a little walk would perhaps be good, mebbe."

"All right, wait till I get my cap," was the unsuspecting reply.

"I think perhaps you won't need it, mebbe. I cherish the opinion you'll perhaps be warm enough." Bill's voice had unconsciously passed into a sterner tone. Hi was on his feet and at the door.

"This here interview is private *and* confidential," Bill said to his partner.

"Exactly," said Hi, opening the door. At this the young fellow, who was a strapping six-footer, but soft and flabby, drew back and refused to go. He was too late. Bill's grip was on his collar and out they went into the snow, and behind them Hi closed the door. In vain the young fellow struggled to wrench himself free from the hands that had him by the shoulder and the back of the neck.

I took it all in from the window. He might have been a boy for all the effect his plungings had upon the long, sinewy arms that gripped him so fiercely. After a minute's furious struggle the young fellow stood quiet, when Bill suddenly shifted his grip from the shoulder to the seat of his buckskin trousers. Then began a series of revolutions—up and down, forward and back, which the unfortunate victim, with hands wildly clutching at empty air, was quite powerless to resist till he was brought up panting and gasping, subdued, to a standstill.

"I'll larn you agnostic and several other kinds of trick," said Bill, in a terrible voice, his drawl lengthening perceptibly. "Come round here, will you, and shove your second-handed trash down our throats?" Bill paused to get words, then, bursting out in rising wrath, "There ain't no sootable words for sich conduct. By the livin' Jeminy . . ." He suddenly swung his prisoner off his feet, lifted him bodily, and held him over his head at arm's length. "I've a notion to . . ."

"Don't! Don't, for heaven's sake!" cried the struggling wretch. "I'll stop it! I will!"

Bill at once lowered him and set him on his feet.

"All right! Shake!" he said, holding out his hand, which the other took with caution.

It was a remarkably sudden conversion and lasting in its effects. There was no more agnosticism in the little group that gathered around the Pilot for the nightly reading.

The interest in the reading kept growing night by night.

"Seems as if the Pilot was gittin' in his work," said Bill to me, and looking at the grave, eager faces, I agreed. He was getting in his work with Bill too, though perhaps Bill did not know it. I remember one night, when the others had gone, the Pilot was reading to us the parable of the talents. Bill was particularly interested in the servant who failed in his duty.

"Ornery cuss, eh?" he remarked. "And gall too, eh? Served him blamed well right, in my opinion!" Then, after a slight hesitation he said, "This here church-buildin' business now, do you think that'll perhaps count, mebbe? I guess not, eh? Tain't much, o' course, anyway."

Poor Bill, he was like a child, and the Pilot handled him with a mother's touch.

"What are you best at, Bill?"

"Bronco bustin' and cattle," answered Bill, "that's my line."

"Well, Bill, my line is preaching just now, and piloting, you know." The Pilot's smile was like a sunbeam on a rainy day, for there were tears in his eyes and voice. "And we have just got to be faithful. You see what He says: 'Well done, good and *faithful* servant. Thou hast been *faithful*.'"

Bill was puzzled. "Faithful!" he repeated. "Does that mean with the cattle, perhaps?"

"Yes, that's just it, Bill, and with everything else that comes your way."

And Bill never forgot that lesson, for I heard him, with a kind of quiet enthusiasm, giving it to Hi as a great find. "Now, I call that a fair deal," he said to his friend. "Gives every man a show. No cards up the sleeve."

"That's so," was Hi's thoughtful reply, "distributes the trumps."

Somehow Bill came to be regarded as an authority on questions of religion and morals. No one ever accused him of "gettin' religion." He went about his work in his slow, quiet way, but he was always sharing his discoveries with "the boys." And if anyone puzzled him with subtleties, he never rested till he had him face-to-face with the Pilot.

And so it came that the Pilot and Bill drew to each other with more than brotherly affection. When Bill got into difficulty with problems that have vexed the souls of men far wiser than he, the Pilot would either disentangle the knots or would turn his mind to the truths that stood out sure and clear, and Bill would be content.

"That's good enough for me," Bill would say, and his heart would be at rest.

22

How the Swan Creek Church Was Opened

Near the end of the year the Pilot fell sick. Bill nursed him like a mother and sent him off to Gwen's for a rest and change, forbidding him to return till the church was finished.

The day of the church opening came, a bright beautiful Christmas Day. The air was still and full of frosty light, and the hills lay asleep under their dazzling coverlets.

The people were all there—farmers, ranchers, cowboys, wives, and children—all happy, all proud of their new church. They all waited expectantly for the Pilot and the Old Timer who were to bring Gwen if the day was fine. As the time passed on, Bill, as master of ceremonies, began to grow uneasy. Then Indian Joe appeared and handed a note to Bill. He read it, grew gray in the face, and passed it to me. Looking, I saw in poor, wavering lines the words, "Dear Bill. Go on with the opening. Sing the psalm, you know the one, and say a prayer, and oh, come to me quick, Bill. Your Pilot."

Bill gradually pulled himself together, announced in a strange voice, "The Pilot can't come," handed me the psalm, and said, "Make them sing."

It was that grand psalm for all hill peoples, "I to the Hills Will Lift Mine Eyes," and with wondering faces they sang the strong, steadying words. After the psalm was over, the people sat and waited. Bill looked at the Honorable Fred Ashley, then at Robbie Muir, then said to me in a low voice, "Kin you make a prayer?"

I shook my head, ashamed as I did so of my cowardice.

Again Bill paused, then said, "The Pilot says there's got to be a prayer. Kin anyone make one?"

Again, dead solemn silence.

Then Hi, who was near the back, spoke up: "What's the matter with you trying, Bill?"

The red began to come up in Bill's white face.

"'Tain't in my line. But the Pilot says there's got to be a prayer, and I'm going to stay with the game." Then, leaning on the pulpit, he said, "Let's pray," and began:

"God Almighty, I ain't no good at this, and perhaps You'll understand if I don't put things right." Then a pause followed, during which I heard some of the women beginning to sob.

"What I want to say," Bill went on, "is, we're mighty glad about this church, which we know it's You and the Pilot that's worked it. And we're all glad to chip in."

Then again he paused, and, looking up, I saw his hard, gray face working and two tears stealing down his cheeks. Then he started again: "But about the Pilot—I don't want to persoom—but if You don't mind, we'd like to have him stay—in fact, don't see how we kin do without him—look at all the boys here; he's just getting his work in and is bringin' 'em right along, and, God Almighty, if You take him away, it might be a good thing for himself, but for us—oh, God," the voice quivered and was silent. "Amen."

Then someone, I think it must have been the Lady Charlotte, began: "Our Father," and all joined that could.

For a few moments Bill stood up, looking at them silently. Then, as if remembering his duty, he said, "This here church is open. Excuse me."

He stood at the door, gave a word of direction to Hi, who had followed him out, and leaping on his bronco shook him into a hard gallop.

The Swan Creek Church was opened. The form of service may not have been correct, but if great love and appealing faith count for anything, then all that was necessary was done.

23

The Pilot's Last Port

In the old times a funeral was regarded in the Swan Creek country as a kind of solemn festivity. In those days, for the most part, men died in their boots and were planted with much honor and loyal libation. There was often neither shroud nor coffin, and in the far West many a poor fellow lies as he fell, wrapped in his own or his comrade's blanket.

It was the manager of the XL Company's ranch that introduced crepe. The occasion was the funeral of one of the ranch cowboys, killed by his bronco. When the pallbearers and mourners appeared with bands and streamers of crepe, this was voted by the majority as "too cheerful." That circumstance alone was enough to render that funeral famous, but it was remembered, too, as having shocked the proprieties in another, more serious manner. No one would be so narrow-minded as to object to the custom of the return procession falling into a series of wild horse races, ending up at Latour's in a general riot. But to race with the corpse was considered bad form.

The "corpse driver," as he was called, could hardly be blamed on this occasion. His acknowledged place was at the head of the procession, and it was a point of honor that that place should be retained. The fault clearly lay with the driver of the XL Ranch sleigh, containing the mourners. These mourners felt aggrieved that Hi Kendal, driving the Ashley team with the pallbearers, should be given the place of honor just behind the corpse driver. The XL driver wanted to know what, in the name of all that was black and blue, the Ashley Ranch had to do with the funeral? Whose was that corpse, anyway? Didn't it belong to the XL Ranch?

Hi, on the other hand, contended that the

corpse was in the charge of the pallbearers. "It was their duty to see it right to the grave, and if they were not on hand, how was it goin' to git there? They didn't expect it would git up and git there by itself, did they?" He "didn't want no mourners foolin' round that corpse till it was properly planted; after that they might git in their work."

But the XL driver could not accept this view, and at the first opportunity slipped past Hi and his pallbearers and took the place next to the sleigh that carried the coffin. It is possible that Hi might have borne this affront and loss of position with an even mind, but the jeering remarks of the mourners as they slid past triumphantly could not be endured, and the next moment the three teams were abreast in a race for dear life. The corpse driver, having the advantage of the beaten track, soon left the other two behind running neck and neck for second place, which was captured finally by Hi and maintained to the graveside.

The whole proceeding was considered quite improper, and at Latour's that night, after full and bibulous discussion, it was agreed that the corpse driver fairly distributed the blame. "For his part," he said, "he knew he hadn't ought to make no corpse git any such move on, but he wasn't goin' to see that there corpse take second place at his own funeral. Not if he could help it. And as for the others, he thought that the pallbearers had a sight more to do with the plantin' than them giddy mourners."

When they gathered at the Meredith ranch to carry out the Pilot to his grave, it was felt that the Foothill Country was called to a new experience. They were all there. The men from the Porcupine and from beyond the fort, the police with the inspector in command, all the farmers for twenty miles around, and of course all the ranchers and cowboys of the Swan Creek country. There was no effort at repression. There was no need, for the cowboys, for the first time in their experience, had no heart for fun. And as they rode up and hitched their horses to the fence, or drove their sleighs into the yard and took off the bells, there was no loud-voiced salutation, but with silent nods they took their places in the crowd about the door or passed into the kitchen.

The men from the Porcupine could not quite understand the gloomy silence. It was something unprecedented in a country where men laughed all care to scorn and saluted death with a nod. But they were quick to read signs, and with characteristic courtesy they fell in with the mood they could not understand.

This was the day of the cowboy's grief. To the rest of the community the Pilot was preacher; to the cowboys he was comrade and friend. They had been slow to admit him to their confidence, but steadily he had won his place with them, till within the last few months they had come to count him as one of themselves. He had ridden the range with the cowboys; he had slept in their shacks and cooked his meals on their tin stoves; and besides, he was Bill's chum. That alone was enough to win him a right to all they owned. The preacher was theirs, and they were only beginning to take full pride in him when he passed out from them, leaving an emptiness in their life new and unexplained.

No man in that country had ever shown concern for the cowboys, nor had it occurred to them that any could, till the Pilot came. It took them long to believe that the interest he showed in them was genuine and not simply professional. Then, too, from a preacher they had expected chiefly pity, warning, and rebuke. The Pilot astonished them by giving them respect, admiration, and open-hearted affection. It was months before they could get over their suspicion that he was trying to pull the wool over their eyes. But once the cowboys did get over their suspicions, they gave him back all the trust and love of their big, generous hearts.

The Pilot had made this world new to some of them, and to all he had given glimpses of the next world. It was no wonder that they stood in dumb groups about the house where the man who had done all this for them and had been all this to them lay dead.

There was no demonstration of grief. The Duke was in command, and his quiet, firm voice, giving directions, helped all to self-control. The women who were gathered in the middle room were weeping quietly. Bill was nowhere to be seen, but near the inner door sat Gwen in her chair, with Lady Charlotte beside her, holding her hand. Gwen's face, worn with long suffering, was pale, but serene as the morning sky, and with not a trace of tears. As my eye caught hers, she beckoned me to her.

"Where's Bill?" she asked. "Bring him in."

I found him at the back of the house.

"Aren't you coming in, Bill?"

"No, I guess there's plenty without me," he responded in his slow way.

"You'd better come in, the service is going to begin," I urged.

"Don't seem as if I cared for to hear anythin' much. I ain't much used to preachin', anyway, 'cept his o' course."

"Come in, Bill," I urged again. "It will look strange, you know."

But Bill replied, "I guess I'll not bother." After a pause he added, "You see, there's them wimmin turnin' on the waterworks, and like as not they'd swamp me sure."

I reported to Gwen, who answered in her old imperious way, "Tell him I want him." I took Bill the message.

"Why didn't you say so before?" He entered the house and took up his position behind Gwen's chair.

Opposite, and leaning against the door, stood the Duke, with a look of quiet earnestness on his handsome face. At his side stood the Honorable Fred Ashley, and behind him the Old Timer, looking bewildered and woe-stricken. The Pilot had filled a large place in the old man's life. The rest of the men stood about the room and filled the kitchen beyond, all quiet, solemn, sad.

In Gwen's room, the one farthest in, lay the Pilot, stately and beautiful under the magic touch of death. And as I stood and looked down on the quiet face, I saw why Gwen shed no tear, but carried a look of serene triumph. She had read the face correctly. The lines of weariness that had been growing so painfully clear the last few months were smoothed out, the look of care was gone, and in place of weariness was the proud smile of victory and peace.

The service was beautiful in its simplicity. The minister, the Pilot's superior, had come out from town to take charge. He was a little man, but sturdy and well set. His face was burned with the suns and frosts he had braved over the years. Still in the prime of his manhood, his hair and beard were grizzled and his face deep-lined, for the toils and cares of a pioneer missionary's life are neither few nor light. But out of his kindly blue eyes looked the heart of a hero, and as he spoke to us we felt the prophet's touch and caught a gleam of the prophet's fire.

"'I have fought a good fight,'" he read. The

ring in his voice lifted up all our heads, and as he pictured to us the life of that battered hero who had written these words, I saw Bill's eyes begin to gleam and his lank figure straighten out its lazy angles. Then he turned the pages quickly and read again, "'Let not your heart be troubled.... In my father's house are many mansions.'"

The minister's voice took a lower, sweeter tone; he looked over our heads and for a few moments spoke of the eternal hope. Then, looking round into the faces turned so eagerly to him, he talked to us of the Pilot—how at first he had sent him to us with fear and trembling—he was so young—but how he had come to trust in him, to rejoice in his work, and to hope much from his life. Now it was all over, but he felt sure his young friend had not given his life in vain. He paused as he looked from one to the other till his eyes rested on Gwen's face. I was startled, as I believe he was too, at the smile that parted her lips, so evidently saying "Yes, but how much better I know than you."

"Yes," he went on, after a pause, answering her smile, "you all know better than I that his work among you will not pass away with his death," and the smile on Gwen's face grew brighter. "And now you must not grudge him his reward and his rest . . . and his home."

And Bill, nodding his head slowly, said under his breath, "That's so."

Then they sang that hymn of the dawning glory of Immanuel's land, Lady Charlotte playing the organ and the Duke leading with clear, steady voice. When they came to the last verse the minister made a sign, and while they waited he read the words:

> I've wrestled on towards heaven
> 'Gainst storm, and wind, and tide.
> And so on to that last victorious cry,—
> I hail the glory dawning
> In Immanuel's Land.

For a moment it looked as if the singing could not go on, for tears were on the minister's face and the women were beginning to sob, but the Duke's clear, quiet voice caught up the song and steadied them all to the end.

After the prayer they all went in and looked at the Pilot's face. Then they filed out, leaving behind only those that knew him best. The Duke and the Honorable Fred stood looking down at the quiet face.

"The country has lost a good man, Duke," said the Honorable Fred. The Duke nodded silently.

Lady Charlotte came and gazed at the Pilot. "Dear, dear Pilot," she whispered, her tears falling fast. "Dear, dear Pilot! Thank God for you! You have done much for me." Then she stooped and kissed him on his cold lips and on his forehead.

Then Gwen seemed to suddenly wake as from a dream. She turned and, looking up in a frightened way, said to Bill, "I want to see him again. Carry me!"

And Bill gathered her up in his arms and took her in. As they looked on the face touched with proud peace and the stateliness of death, Gwen's fear passed away. But when the Duke moved to cover the face, Gwen drew a sharp breath and, clinging to Bill, said with a sudden gasp, "Oh, Bill, I can't bear it alone. I'm afraid."

She was thinking of the long, weary days of pain before her that she must face now without the Pilot's touch and smile and voice.

"Me too," said Bill, thinking of the days before him. He could have said nothing better. Gwen looked in his face a moment, then said, "We'll help each other," and Bill, swallowing hard, could only nod his head in reply. Once more they leaned down and looked at the Pilot, and then Gwen said quietly, "Take me away, Bill," and he carried her into the outer room.

Turning back, I caught a look on the Duke's face so full of grief that I could not help showing my amazement. He noticed and said, "The best man I ever knew. He had done something for me too. . . . I'd give the world to die like that."

Then he covered the face.

We sat at Gwen's window, Bill, with Gwen in his arms, and I, watching. Down the sloping, snow-covered hill wound the procession of sleighs and horsemen, without sound of voice or jingle of bell till, one by one, they passed out of our sight and dipped down into the canyon.

Out where the canyon opened to the sunny, sloping prairie they would lay the Pilot to rest, within touch of the canyon he loved. And there he lies to this time. But spring has come many times to the canyon since that winter day and has called to the sleeping flowers, summoning them forth in merry troops, and ever more and more till the canyon ripples with them. And lives are like flowers. In dying they abide not alone, but sow themselves and bloom again with each returning spring.

Often during the following years as I came upon someone from those Foothill days, I would catch a glimpse in word and deed and look of him we called, first in jest, but afterwards with true and tender affection, our Sky Pilot.

About the Author

Ralph Connor (1860–1937) was a pioneer missionary pastor who began his career ministering in the small communities of the Canadian Rockies. He began writing his experiences and those of other missionaries of Western Canada in a series of articles first published in a church magazine. They became so popular that he put them into a book and subsequently wrote a series of novels on the lives of the men and women who settled the Canadian West. He traveled and lectured throughout North America, Australia, and New Zealand. His books have sold over five million copies.

About the Editor

Timothy McCullough was born in Minnesota and received a degree in history from Mankato State University. He taught high school history for a number of years before entering the Christian bookselling industry in 1981. He is now an educator and marketing consultant. McCullough lives in suburban Atlanta, Georgia with his wife and two children.